A CORNISH SUMMER'S KISS

JO BARTLETT

First published in Great Britain in 2021 by Boldwood Books Ltd.

Copyright © Jo Bartlett, 2021

Cover Design by CC Book Design

Cover photography: Shutterstock

The moral right of Jo Bartlett to be identified as the author of this work has been asserted in accordance with the Copyright, Designs and Patents Act 1988.

All rights reserved. No part of this book may be reproduced in any form or by any electronic or mechanical means, including information storage and retrieval systems, without written permission from the author, except for the use of brief quotations in a book review.

This book is a work of fiction and, except in the case of historical fact, any resemblance to actual persons, living or dead, is purely coincidental.

Every effort has been made to obtain the necessary permissions with reference to copyright material, both illustrative and quoted. We apologise for any omissions in this respect and will be pleased to make the appropriate acknowledgements in any future edition.

A CIP catalogue record for this book is available from the British Library.

Paperback ISBN 978-1-80048-981-3

Large Print ISBN 978-1-80048-980-6

Hardback ISBN 978-1-80048-979-0

Ebook ISBN 978-1-80048-983-7

Kindle ISBN 978-1-80048-982-0

Audio CD ISBN 978-1-80048-974-5

MP3 CD ISBN 978-1-80048-975-2

Digital audio download ISBN 978-1-80048-977-6

Boldwood Books Ltd
23 Bowerdean Street
London SW6 3TN
www.boldwoodbooks.com

*For the friends and family who make high days and holidays so special,
you know who you are xx*

1

Maybe it had been a mistake to rent Myrtle Cottage. Even getting there was suddenly terrifying. It was just four walls, but it held so many memories of a time when life was good. Back then Lexie had often willed something to happen, something to shake things up. Be careful what you wish for, they said. How true that had turned out to be.

The tide was closing in and, any minute now, the stretch of beach that provided the only access to the cottage would disappear beneath the waves. Lexie eased the car off the concrete ramp and onto the sand. She was used to sitting bumper-to-bumper in traffic – a city driver, perfectly capable of racing for the last parking space and leaning heavily on the horn if someone cut her up – but this was different. Finn had always driven when they were down here and somehow the twisting Cornish roads were making her more nervous than London ever had.

Holding her breath as the tyres touched the sand, she half expected them to start spinning, leaving her hopelessly stranded at the edge of the water. Only the car didn't stop, it glided effortlessly across the beach as though there'd been no change in the surface at all.

'Okay Albie, we're going to make it.' She reached out a hand and a wet brown nose gave her a reassuring nudge. 'We'll be all right here, just the two of us, won't we?' Another nudge from the Labrador, curled up on the passenger seat beside her, was all the reassurance she needed.

* * *

As she brought the last bag in from the car, a shadow moved at the corner of Lexie's eye and for a moment she could have sworn it was him – Finn – standing there in the room, laughing at their good fortune that the cottage should have become unexpectedly free, and for two whole months at that. It was just a trick of the light, of course, not something she could reach out and touch. Finn was gone and, even two years in, it still twisted her insides every time she forced herself to admit it.

'I don't suppose the bride thought it was good luck.' Lexie spoke aloud, in part to Albie – who briefly acknowledged her with a raise of his soft golden head, before going back to sniffing the unfamiliar skirting board – and in part to the empty space where her husband's presence seemed to hang.

'Just imagine being in her shoes, jilted a fortnight before the wedding and a six week honeymoon going to waste!' It was what the agent from the holiday company had told her when she'd inquired about the cottage on a whim one wet Wednesday afternoon; when the longing to be somewhere she and Finn had spent so much time alone together had almost overwhelmed her. 'Poor girl.' The woman from Cornish Gems, whose name was Ailsa, had confided over the phone. 'Must be the worst thing that can happen to a woman, being jilted, don't you think?'

Lexie had barely resisted the urge to put the woman straight, to tell her that there were far worse things that could happen than narrowly escaping a marriage to someone who clearly didn't love you anyway, but she didn't. She'd discovered in the time since Finn had been gone that most people didn't want to hear what you *really* had to say, even when they seemed to be asking.

'Sounds terrible.' Lexie had given the expected reply instead, before moving the conversation on. 'Did you say it's available for six weeks?'

'Well, they're both teachers, you see.' Ailsa was getting into her stride now, as if regaling a plot from a TV soap. 'She had it all planned, a romantic summer in Cornwall. And in Port Kara of all places – there's always the chance of bumping into a royal down there these days, you know! But she's going to the Canaries with her bridesmaids instead and, if I can rent it out again, she won't lose the hefty deposit she's paid. I'm sure it would be a huge weight off her mind.'

'I'll take the whole six weeks.' The words had come out of Lexie's mouth almost as if someone else had spoken them. She hadn't planned on going away for anything like as long as that. Although what was stopping her? She'd sold the restaurant and the one thing that didn't keep her awake at night was worrying about money. Finn had seen to that.

'That's amazing!' The excitement in Ailsa's voice went flat as quickly as it had arrived. 'Although you do realise it's *completely* cut off to vehicles at high tide? All the other cottages in Port Kara rent out without even advertising them, since it became such a celebrity hotspot, but Myrtle Cottage…'

'I've stayed there before.' Lexie crossed the fingers on her left hand as she spoke, praying that Ailsa wouldn't demand as much of her life story as she clearly had the jilted bride's.

'Well that's fantastic then and it's free the middle two weeks of

September at the moment, straight after your stay, if you wanted to make it a full two months?'

'In for a penny.' The brittle laugh caught in Lexie's throat. She reeled off her credit card details before she could change her mind. Ailsa hadn't questioned her further; she was just relieved, it seemed, that the poor jilted bride wouldn't suffer any more. Some people had all the luck.

* * *

Elliott loved the early evening during the summer months, especially when it coincided with high tide and the tourists had cleared the beach. It was as if he owned the whole world looking out to sea from the top of the cliff face. He'd finished with the guests for the day, done more than his fair share of coaxing and cajoling nervous townies to do something adventurous, to take advantage of the activities they'd paid a high price for, but which, more often than not, terrified them in practice. Now it was his turn for a bit of adventure. The cliffs on this part of the headland were too sheer for any of his guests to attempt – even those who were on a return visit and had long since caught the adrenaline bug.

The rocks beneath the cliff face at Dagger's Head rose up from the water like the jagged teeth of a giant, waiting to impale their victim. Further to the left were a series of rocky outcrops, inaccessible on foot, as they were now interspersed with narrow gaps on the old coastal path that seemed to erode further with every turn of the tide. Only an Olympic long jumper could navigate the track now, and even then, they'd risk plunging onto the rocks below. It was what Elliott liked best about the climb down the rock face and along the old coastal path – before he made his way back up the cliff further along using grappling irons – the absolute certainty that he wouldn't be disturbed. It wasn't that he didn't enjoy company but, after spending all day being sociable, solitude definitely had its appeal.

When he saw her, he almost lost his footing. He was so shocked at the sight of her navigating the crumbling pathway that, had he been the type to believe in all that, he might have thought she'd emerged from the sea itself. With her long blonde hair falling in soft waves below her shoulders, there was definitely something of the mermaid about her. Still, the fact that she was wearing jeans and appeared to be chasing a sandy coloured Labrador along the path, put an end to that particular illusion. The reality was that she was in danger of slipping and there was nowhere to go but down, onto rocks that would cut her to ribbons, and a sea that was far crueller than it looked, even on a warm summer's evening. A light breeze carried her shout up to Elliott, who was already moving as swiftly as he could towards her. She must having been calling the dog, Alfie or Albie, he couldn't quite make it out. The animal would be much more sure-footed than her, though, and she was taking a stupid risk running to try and catch it.

He looked down just in time to see the dog leap over a gap in the old coastal path, its front paws landing squarely on the other side, but its back legs falling short for a moment and scrabbling against the loose surface beneath. Elliott held his breath but kept moving towards the mystery woman all the time. No matter how ridiculous it was, he had a horrible premonition she was going to try to follow the dog across. Her voice was clearer now, the Labrador's name was definitely Albie and she was almost screaming it, her distress undeniable.

For a few more seconds the dog's back legs scrabbled desperately against the unstable surface, but somehow it managed to secure enough momentum to safely get all four paws onto the path itself. Elliott finally released his breath and tried calling out to the woman below, to warn her not to follow the dog whatever she did.

He shouted, his voice bouncing off the rock face, but she didn't even look up, the sound of the waves crashing against the rocks beneath her clearly drowning him out.

She was calling Albie to come back across the gap in the pathway to her and, as he got closer still, he could make out her face – pale with terror. He knew what she was going to do and he was powerless to stop it. She wouldn't respond to his shouts, or wait for him to get there and help, because she had no idea he was on his way. The dog, on the other side of the gap, gingerly approached the edge he'd just scrabbled over, looked down and turned round again, whining loudly so that Elliott could hear, even from thirty feet or so away.

He was so close; she must be able hear him now. He shouted again, just a simple but meaningful 'No!' this time, but still she didn't look up. The dog clearly wasn't willing to come back across the gap, and Elliott tried desperately to get to the woman before she did something really stupid. It was as if they were both moving in slow motion, him descending down the last twenty feet or so of the rock towards the old coastal path, and her stepping off the pathway to try and breach the gap to the dog. He didn't take his eyes off her, convinced that if he held her in his gaze he could keep her safe until he got there, and he almost lost his own footing because of it.

She stepped off, when he was so close it felt as though he could almost have reached out and stopped her, but he was still about ten feet away. He heard the scream, close enough now to see the fear flicker in her eyes. He was sure she was going to disappear into the gap and that he'd have to watch her fall, live with that on his conscience forever. But, somehow, she managed to grab hold of something, an old tree root or maybe a large tuft of reed, although how long it would hold her weight was anyone's guess.

'Don't move, not even to look up at me, it might be enough to snap whatever it is you're holding on to.' He was just above her now, on the rock face. He might have enjoyed the adrenaline surge of the fast-paced free climb down the cliff in other circumstances. The sort of risk his old friends would insist he only took because he missed the thrill of the chase since quitting London and a highly pressured job, which showed just how little they really knew him. Not today though; putting his own life in danger was one thing, he was an expert and it was always a carefully measured risk, just enough to make things interesting. Watching someone else do it, and totally recklessly too, was anything but fun.

'I don't think I can hold on any more.' Her voice was small, as if even talking was an effort.

'You can do it; just a few more seconds. Don't talk though, just hold on.'

Taking a grappling iron out of his rucksack, he secured it as swiftly as he could, trying to keep calm as he threaded the climbing rope through it, able now to make out the panicked breathing of the woman just below him and the whining of the dog on the ledge to his left.

Securing the rope around his waist, he reached down, grabbing her wrist. 'You're going to need to let go of whatever you're holding on to, and trust me.'

'I'm scared.'

'I know, but I promise you're going to be okay; I've got you now. What's your name?'

'Lexie. Lexie Turner.'

'Okay, Lexie, we're going to do this. You can trust me, there's no way I'll let anything happen to you.' He'd keep hold of her, or die trying. Slowly, she uncurled her fingers from what he could now see was a thick clump of reed roots. Someone must have been watching out for her – for that to hold her, and for Elliott to be in the right place at just the moment she'd decided to do something as crazy as she had. It wasn't her time and he'd make sure of it. 'That's it, now lift up your left arm too, so I can take hold of your other wrist.'

Pulling her up towards him was hard and the muscles in his arms strained against the pressure, but finally they were face to face, the scent of her perfume ridiculously at odds with the seriousness of the situation. He wrapped the rope around her waist – she was going nowhere now.

'Thank you.' When he looked into her eyes this time, there was something else there, something unreadable. Whatever it was, there was real sadness, and for the first time he wondered if she'd risked her life on purpose. Surely no one would do something that crazy without some sort of death wish?

'Is Albie okay?' Her eyes darted towards the dog, flat against the cliff face, still whining.

'He's fine. Let me get you onto the safe part of the path first and then we'll worry about the dog. I'm Elliott by the way.' He laughed then, at the absurdity of their introduction, glad to break the tension. The intensity in her eyes when she'd asked about the dog had been too much to take.

* * *

Lexie had never been so glad to feel the stability of the ground beneath her feet, as Elliott manoeuvred them both onto the safe side of the path, which Albie had leapt from. She thanked whatever it was – fate, pure good luck or something else – that had put him on the cliff face at just the moment she'd decided to do something so ridiculous.

Her decision making had hardly been rational since she'd lost Finn, and Albie was all that she had left of him – he'd been their baby, whilst they waited until they were ready to have one of their own, never knowing that time would run out first – so she couldn't lose him too. Yet despite the sheer torture of the two years since Finn's death and the times when she'd wished she could join him, dangling over that ledge she'd been sure of one thing – she wanted to live, even without the husband she'd lost far too soon.

'Thank you.' The words seemed inadequate for what he'd done, but she couldn't help asking for more. 'Albie…'

'It's okay, I'm going for him now.' Elliott gave her a reassuring smile, his deep brown eyes crinkling slightly in the corners as he did. He made a pretty good hero. He definitely looked the part and he'd had the strength to haul her up to safety, too. She doubted he'd have been able to do it if Finn had been alive; she'd eaten far too well back then and running a restaurant together had put temptation in her path. But, eating, like most things, had lost its appeal without Finn and now she was far too thin according to her well-meaning parents. As it turned out, being skinny for once in her life had probably saved her from plunging onto the rocks. Although there was no denying it was Elliott who was really responsible for that.

'Thanks. I know it's a lot to ask, when you've already rescued me, but stupid as it seems that disobedient dog means the world to me.'

'It's not stupid at all. Trying to leap across a gap that big,' Elliott paused and looked into the water below them, 'now that's stupid. Although I'd probably choose a much stronger word than that.'

Before she had a chance to reply, he began to climb back up the rock face, crossing the gap she'd tried to breach a few feet above where she was standing. He looked like a professional, with all the right gear for climbing, and she knew Albie was in safe hands.

Like most Labradors, Albie was friendly and would usually do anything for a treat, but his experience in the last twenty minutes or so had clearly brought out the coward in him and he almost shrank into the cliffside as Elliott strapped some sort of harness onto him.

Barking in protest as his rescuer hoisted him upwards, Albie's legs paddled in thin air like a character from a cartoon.

Once Lexie started to laugh, she couldn't stop. Relief, shock and a whole gamut of emotions, which sat far too close to the surface these days, threatened to overwhelm her.

'Are you okay?' Elliott placed a hand on her arm. All she could do was nod, through a mix of tears and laughter, as he picked up the lead she'd dropped, when she'd tried to follow Albie, and clipped it onto the dog's collar before taking off the harness. 'I'm not taking any chances with Houdini here.'

'That's probably a wise move. I think being out of the city for once just went to his head, *to both of our heads*. I should never have let him off, or taken this path. It's just so different from when we were last here.' A look of relief swept across his face as she spoke.

'I did wonder if you were...' He paused for a second. 'Sorry, now I'm the one being stupid. It's not as if you'd take a dog with you if you were planning to jump, is it?' He had a disarming smile and his accent wasn't typically local, although the even tan and the blond tips to his otherwise dark hair meant he wouldn't have looked out of place striding into the surf. She shook her head at the thought; surfing was Finn's first love and if she wanted to pretend to Elliott that everything was okay, she had to keep thoughts of her husband at least partially at bay.

'No, I definitely wasn't planning on it. Not with the price I've paid to rent Myrtle Cottage for the whole summer. It would be a real waste to end it all on day one.' She laughed a bit too hard at the feeble joke, but Elliott smiled again, patting Albie's head as he nudged at his rescuer's legs.

'It's a quaint little place. A bit lonely perhaps, when the tide cuts it off, but it's a honeymooner's paradise.' His eyes flickered towards her left hand, where her wedding and engagement rings still sat, allowing her to keep up the pretence that she still had Finn.

'I'm not on honeymoon, I'm...' She'd been about to use the dreaded word *widowed*, but she didn't want to see that look on his face, the mixture of pity and embarrassment everyone seemed to get at the mention of it. Being widowed so young somehow made other people really uncomfortable. 'It's just me and Albie. That's why I had to rescue him, I'm never lonely with him about.' The tears that stung her eyes were unexpected, but Elliott really had no idea what he'd done for her.

'I'd say it's nice to meet you, Lexie, but I'm not sure that's appropriate given the circumstances. Are you okay to get back down to the cottage by yourself, or do you want me to walk with you?'

'We'll be fine, because of you. I'm sorry to have interrupted your climb, but so thankful to whatever fate it was that put you here tonight. What are the odds of an expert climber being on hand, just when you need one?' She laughed again, thankful that he hadn't questioned her further about being on her own; she wasn't sure she was up to explaining what had happened to Finn.

'With me, the odds are pretty good around here. I run the adventure centre, up on the cliff top and this is the sort of thing I do for relaxation.' It was his turn to laugh, in response to the expression she knew must have crossed her face. 'It's no problem, just promise me you won't try anything like that again. If it's been a while since you stayed, the old coastal path has been really damaged over the past year or so and there's none of it that's really safe any more.'

'I promise, but if there's ever anything I can do to pay you back, just say the word.' She kissed his cheek, the warmth and slight tang of salt on his skin stirring another memory.

'I'm just glad you're both all right. Stay safe, okay? And maybe head up to Dorton's Adventure Centre whilst you're here, so you can learn about the coastal paths that *are* safe to follow, and what to do when you get into trouble. At least that way I'll be able to sleep at night!'

'I might just take you up on that.' Lexie watched as he raised a hand in response, already heading back up the cliffside. He was definitely a pro.

The walk back down to the cottage was blissfully uneventful and even the irrepressibly excitable Albie was subdued. Despite her assurance to Elliott that she and Albie would never be lonely, the quiet back inside Myrtle Cottage was painful. It was probably just the drama of almost plunging between the cliffs into the sea, but closing her eyes – with Albie's head on her feet, as she sunk into an armchair – the usual visions of Finn were interspersed with Elliott's face and a new emotion bubbled to the surface. Guilt.

2

The screeching of a seagull woke Lexie just after 8 a.m. It would have seemed absurdly late back in the days when she'd run the restaurant, rising at 5 a.m. and heading to the markets at least three times a week to pick up fresh produce. Back then, sleeplessness had never been something that had plagued her. The long hours spent on her feet and the frenetic pace of running one of the most successful restaurants in their part of London had been enough to ward off insomnia. There'd always been Finn's solid back to cuddle into, too – a safe haven even on the occasional nights when she was worried about something stupid, like getting their tax returns in on time. All those sorts of worries seemed so trivial now that Finn was gone.

Stretching, Lexie forced herself to throw back the covers. Albie, who'd been lying on a rug by the side of her bed, got to his feet, his thick-set tail thudding against the wall of the bedroom.

'Sorry boy, I bet you're desperate for a walk and your breakfast, aren't you?' He looked up at her, total trust in his eyes – he needed her as much as she needed him. 'I'll let you out for a bit and then we can have a proper walk after we've eaten.' Was it insane to talk to a dog quite as often as she talked to Albie? It was hard luck if it was, they were a team now. The one solid presence left in her world.

* * *

'Morning.' She'd barely stepped outside the door of the cottage, with Albie on his lead, when another dog walker raised his hand in greeting and called out. She waved and nodded in response, dipping her head before he could strike up a conversation. It was strange how friendly dog walkers were, even in London where people were usually head down and hell-bent on getting to their own destination. It completely changed when you had a dog with you. She'd had conversations walking Albie on Hampstead Heath, where some of the other dog walkers had revealed more about their personal lives than she knew about some of her closest friends. But Lexie always kept her head down these days.

Despite a cloudless sky, the wind was strong enough to whip up the surf and there were already a few wetsuit-clad surfers heading out with their boards. How long would it take before she stopped expecting one of them to be Finn?

'Come on, Alb, let's head into town and see if there's a market on today.' She missed so much of her old life, even the mixture of pressure and excitement that came from cooking for a restaurant full of diners with sky-high expectations. It was nothing like the wrenching emptiness of missing Finn, but it had all been tied up with their life together. Coming back to Cornwall was about letting go of the things she'd been clinging to for the two years since his death. She hadn't been able to go on holiday, or do the job she'd loved for so long, without him by her side. She'd barely been able to function at first, and happiness was a memory she couldn't quite conjure up any more – like chasing a rainbow that just kept moving farther away.

There was magic in Port Kara though, and watching Albie bounce along the edge of the shoreline, where the dying waves finally broke and turned over, she felt alive. It wasn't happiness, exactly, but it was the closest she'd felt to it for a long time.

Leaving the beach, she was careful to stick to the well-signposted new coastal path, after Elliott's warnings from the day before. As a couple about her age walked towards her, stopping to kiss, Lexie caught her breath. Stepping back, the man pushed a strand of hair away from his companion's face. Did they realise how lucky they were, in that moment, when everything in their world was right? Lexie hadn't, not until it was far too late. They didn't speak as she passed by, not even to offer a good morning, too engrossed in each other to notice the woman with tears in her eyes.

As they made their way down to the harbour, Lexie's mood lifted again. The charming hilly streets of Port Kara, leading them to their destination, were weaving their spell, just as they always had. She had to expect ups and downs, everyone had told her that. But being back in Port Kara made it seem possible that, one day, the ups would finally outweigh the downs again.

As she passed the jewellery shop where Finn had bought her some Cornish pearl earrings for the last wedding anniversary they'd spent together, she gripped Albie's lead all the tighter. It was bittersweet being here without him, but she just had to push through the moments when a memory caught her off guard and left her winded.

'Are you in a hurry, my love?' A woman who looked to be in her late sixties stepped out onto the pavement in front of Lexie, as she headed past the row of shops housed in the Victorian arches, which had once been home to ship chandlers and supply stores. Most of them were now trendy independent boutiques and bistros, but the shop the woman stood in front of was narrow, and only slightly wider than the large wooden door emblazoned with the words *Trelawney's Fortunes*.

'I'm not interested, thanks.'

'That's not what I asked, I asked if you were in a hurry.' The woman, who was wearing a dark blue headscarf covered in hundreds of tiny gold stars, smiled at Lexie. She was tempted just to dip her head and rush past, but something stopped her. It wasn't that she found it hard to say no to unwanted sales patters, she was adept at politely refusing the leaflets that were regularly thrust towards her when she walked around London after all. But the woman had such a kind face and she reminded Lexie of Finn's grandmother, who'd died a few months after their wedding, so she couldn't bring herself to just ignore her.

'I'm just walking my dog, so I'm not rushing, but I'm sorry I don't really believe in fortune tellers, and it makes me a bit uncomfortable.'

'I can understand that. But, despite what you say, you seem in a hurry to me and I just think you should slow down.' The woman held out her hand, she had at least two rings on every finger and glittery nail polish that caught the sunlight, matching the twinkle in her eyes.

'I'll bear that in mind.'

'Please do my love, otherwise you'll miss what's right in front of you.' She pressed a card into Lexie's hand as she spoke.

'Thank you.' Closing her fingers around the card, Lexie wondered how long it would be before she could throw it into a litter bin, out of view of the well-meaning but clearly deranged woman still standing in front of her.

'They'd want you to be happy you know.' The woman stepped back and Lexie's head shot up in response. She was obviously just grasping at straws, like those fake fortune tellers in the exposé videos on YouTube did, but she'd touched a nerve all the same.

'Who would?'

'The one you're rushing away from. But you do need to slow down or the thing you'll rush right into won't be right for you.'

'Okay.' Lexie let go of the breath that had caught in her throat. The woman was obviously talking nonsense, guessing that Lexie was on the rebound from a bad relationship and trying to make out she had some sort of psychic power. She had the bad relationship bit wrong for a start. Then there was the idea that she might rush straight into something else; even two years on from Finn's death that was the last thing on her mind. If the woman had been able to tell her what she should be doing next to fill her days with work again, or whether the thought that had flashed into her head about moving away from London permanently was completely crazy, then maybe Lexie would have been tempted to stop and listen to what she had to say, even if she did think it was all just made up rubbish.

'Take care my love and remember not to rush anything. You know where to find me if you want to talk.'

This time Lexie didn't answer and she didn't care if the woman saw her when she tossed the card into the nearest litter bin. This was one part of Port Kara she wouldn't be coming back to.

* * *

The rest of the walk passed without incident and the familiar streets of Port Kara soon lifted her spirits again. Aside from the unwanted attentions of the fortune teller, it was good to be back. Stopping for breakfast in the little café that had always been Finn's favourite, two streets away from the harbour, she'd discovered that the couple who ran it still remembered her name. Albie had even been given his own plate with bacon scraps and a whole sausage. They'd asked where Finn was, which meant explaining the accident again, but when they'd insisted on waiving the bill, she'd almost cried. It was another reminder of why she and Finn had loved Port Kara so much; it had always felt like a place she could call home, if her whole life hadn't been so tied up with living in London.

Walking back towards Myrtle Cottage after breakfast, she was just drawing level with one of the wooden jetties that abutted the harbour wall when a boat chugged in to moor. A group of men and women were on board, all of them wearing wet suits and there was a big pile of diving equipment on one side of the deck.

'Well, I must say, it's a relief to see you sticking to the safety of the harbour this morning. No more cliff jumping for you and Albie!' She recognised Elliott's voice, even before she looked up.

'Doing that once is a mistake anyone could have made. Doing it twice would be foolish.' She returned his smile, despite a twinge of annoyance that he'd brought her stupid mistake up again. Although seeing as she and Albie owed him their lives, this was no time to hold a grudge. 'Looks like you were out diving early this morning?'

'The forecast said the wind was going to pick up, so I knew we'd get the best of the weather that way. Some of this lot haven't quite found their sea legs yet, and, even in the better weather, the journey back to Port Kara was a bit rough for one or two of them'

'Not everyone's an action hero.'

'Are you making fun of me, Mrs Turner?' He smiled more broadly this time, revealing perfectly even teeth. The fact that he'd remembered her name pleased her more than it should. He ran adventure holidays for a living, so he was probably used to learning the names of whole groups of people within minutes of meeting them. It didn't mean anything, and she didn't want it to.

'I just meant that not everyone has your physical capabilities.' Her words were coming out all wrong. Why hadn't she just rushed past the boat, instead of stopping to speak to him? He thought she was an idiot and getting tongue-tied with embarrassment because of it wouldn't help to change his opinion.

'Well, I'll take that as a compliment, I think.' Elliott grinned again, finding her ability to tie herself up in knots far too amusing for her liking. 'How about you? Can I interest you in a diving trip later in the week?'

'God, no! I always stuck to dry land when my husband hit the surf; he couldn't even persuade me to try body boarding, let alone diving. There's something about the sea that's always scared me, even before...'

'Before what?' He was waiting for her to finish a sentence she'd never intended to start, the group around him beginning to gather up their stuff and get off the boat, whilst he kept his eyes firmly fixed on her. She had to say something or he might just stand there, staring at her all day. She'd never been good at making things up on the spot, anyway, so she had to get it over with.

'My husband, Finn, had a surfing accident. He'd gone away with some friends to surf in South Africa for a week.' There was something about Elliott that made her say things she'd rather have kept to herself. Maybe it was the way he went quiet, waiting for a response, until she was desperate to fill the silence. 'He'd always wanted to go, and I bought him the trip for his thirtieth birthday, otherwise he'd never have been there.' She dug her nails into the palms of her hands – going down that path again would kill her too; it had taken months of counselling to stop her fixating on *what ifs*.

'You don't need to tell me if you don't want to.' Elliott's voice was reassuring, the way it had been on the cliff the night before, when he'd promised he wouldn't let her fall.

'It's okay.' Suddenly she wanted to tell him. He clearly thought she was reckless, after the way she'd acted the night before, but maybe this would help him understand. 'Finn was out surfing early in the morning with two of his friends. I'd made him promise he wouldn't take any stupid risks, like going out surfing by himself.'

Elliott had moved closer to her, as the skipper tied the back of the boat to the mooring post. The rest of the guests and crew were already getting drinks from a wooden kiosk to the right of where she stood, their laughter intermittingly rising with the breeze that was still picking up pace. Elliott probably couldn't wait to get away, he had guests to get back to after all, and there she was wittering on. She should just say it, blurt it out, tell this stranger who'd saved her life just how much she wished he'd been around when her husband had needed the same sort of help, and nobody had been there until it was already too late.

'He kept his promise not to take the risks we'd talked about. The waves weren't even that big, he'd surfed in much rougher seas, but he was knocked off his board and hit his head on a rock just below the surface of the water that none of them had known was there. It was several minutes before his friends realised he hadn't resurfaced, but as soon as they did they got him back to the beach. They tried CPR, the lifeguards did too, for twenty minutes until the paramedics reached him, but it was too late.'

'Oh God, I'm so sorry. And here I am running my mouth off about you coming diving; I never did know when to shut up.'

'It's not your fault, how were you supposed to know? I can't expect to avoid every mention of the sea, especially not in a place like Port Kara.'

'It does seem an odd choice to come to a surfer's paradise.' He shook his head. 'I'm sorry. Shall I take my size ten feet out of my mouth and just disappear? It's none of my business why you wanted to come here.'

'It was our go-to place whenever we managed a few days off.' She smiled at the memory. It hadn't been nearly as often as she'd wanted it to be. Running the restaurant had meant they'd had to take a lot of holidays separately, but at least they'd made the time they had together count. It was one of the things she'd always been grateful for, having such a good team at the restaurant, so they'd managed to snatch *some* time alone. She wouldn't have made it through the past couple of years if she hadn't had that thought to cling on to; without it she'd have drowned. 'I used to walk Albie for miles, then sit and paint, whilst Finn surfed. But we'd spend the rest of the time together, not doing much at all. Just being together was enough, do you know what I mean?'

'I can guess, but I've never had that sort of relationship.'

'I find that hard to believe.'

'That, I'll definitely take as a compliment.' He smiled again, making it even harder to believe that he'd never been in love; there must have been plenty of women in Port Kara lining up to change that. The action hero bit probably appealed to most of them too. But not her, not any more. Even if her heart hadn't been shattered into a million tiny pieces that she had no idea how to put back together, she couldn't ever date someone like Elliott. Someone who got his kicks – and made his living – from chasing an adrenaline rush. If she ever worked out how to let herself feel anything for another man, she was going to choose someone safe and steady. A mister nine-to-five, whose idea of adventure was marathoning four seasons of a show on Netflix in a single weekend. That person, if he ever existed, would never hold as much of her heart in his hands as Finn had – she didn't want to risk that again – but at least her patchwork heart would keep beating that way.

'That's good, because it was meant as a compliment. Thanks for listening, and thanks again for last night, but I'd better get going.' She smiled as a pretty redhead standing by the kiosk called out Elliott's name for the third time. 'I think your public are getting impatient.'

'What are your plans for the day?' Elliott clearly wasn't in any hurry to respond to the woman calling his name. He'd just held up his hand and given her a nod, indicating that he'd be there in a minute.

'Albie and I were just going to have a wander around Port Kara to familiarise ourselves with the place again and see what else has changed since our last visit. Apart from the old coastal path disappearing of course.' The roots of her hair prickled at the memory of how stupid she'd been, and how close she'd come to losing Albie as a result.

'How long has it been since you were last here?'

'Almost three years.' It might as well have been a lifetime.

'Well, there's definitely somewhere you need to check out then. Port Kara won an international award last year for the fish market which opened at the west end of the harbour. The scallops are the freshest you'll ever taste and I guarantee you won't be disappointed, if you like seafood that is?'

'Are you on commission?' Lexie raised her eyebrows, glad they were back on safe ground. Food was one thing she could *always* talk about.

'Sadly not, although the way my chef spends money there, I think I should probably get some shares in the business.' Elliott finally stepped off the boat and fell into an easy stride beside her, as they drew level with the kiosk where his guests were still waiting. He patted the shoulder of another man standing on the edge of the group. 'Great dive everyone and there should be some really good footage on the Go Pro when we get back to the centre. I'll leave you in Greg's capable hands, I'm just going to take my friend Lexie up to the market and show her around.'

'You don't have to.' Lexie had no intention of going anywhere with Elliott, and she hadn't missed the daggered look the redhead had thrown in her direction. 'Anyway, what am I going to do with Albie? I couldn't be responsible for what he might do if he got within two hundred metres of a stall of fresh fish. You've seen how he can jump.'

'I have indeed.' Elliott bent down to stroke the dog's head. 'And we definitely don't want a repeat of that. You could tie him up outside, though.'

'I couldn't risk it.' Lexie's voice cracked and the redhead shot her another look. She couldn't expect other people to understand just how precious Albie was, and that she'd truthfully rather die than have anything happen to him. Elliott already knew it, though.

'Of course not.' He touched her arm. 'But we'll only be ten minutes and Greg can keep an eye on Albie for you, just while we have a quick look around.'

'I couldn't ask him to do that.' She didn't want to either.

'Greg's my right hand man.' Elliott clapped a hand on the other man's shoulder again. 'You'll guard Albie with your life, won't you mate?'

'My pleasure.' Greg glanced in her direction and nodded, leaving her no real choice unless she wanted to look like the crazy dog lady of Port Kara.

'So that's a deal then?' Elliott was watching her again.

'Okay, why not.' She desperately tried to keep her tone casual, even though a big part of her wanted to run back to the safety of Myrtle Cottage, taking the dog with her. Forcing herself to hand Albie's lead to Greg, she followed Elliott along the harbour side, determined not to look back.

* * *

Elliott had been only too aware of the way Janey Summers had looked at him and it was clear she'd decided they were going to sleep together from the moment she'd arrived at the adventure centre. Glaston's, the insurance firm she worked for, would potentially be a very lucrative corporate client to land, and they could bring a lot of business to the centre, organising adventure weekends and team building sessions for their staff. But if she was hoping for anything other than a business relationship, then she was out of luck.

He'd heard Janey screaming at her PA about something over breakfast; the poor bloke had looked as if he'd wanted the ground to open up and swallow him. He'd seen that sort of bullying too many times before, passed off under the guise of being tough in business. His father, Charles, was a master at it, and he'd made it all too clear that Elliott's desire to be nothing like him was one of his biggest failures. Although, in the end, his failures had been too numerous to count, according to Charles Dorton. Elliott had lived a lie for far too long but, despite what his father thought, he'd made more money in fifteen years than most people made in a lifetime. Sinking it all into Dorton's Adventure Centre might have been idiotic, in his father's eyes, but he was a million times happier in Cornwall than he'd ever been in London. Turning his back on the potential of earning a seven figure salary had been easy, when it meant saying goodbye to so many phoney people too. It had been a dog-eat-dog world, and most of his colleagues would have happily stabbed him in the back to get one over on him in a business deal. There wasn't enough money in the world to persuade him to go back to following in his father's corporate footsteps, so Janey Summers didn't interest him one bit.

'You don't have to babysit me, you know. I don't make a habit of needing my life saved and I'm pretty sure I can find the fish market all on my own.' Lexie narrowed her eyes as she spoke and set her shoulders back. Even pulling herself up to her full height, she couldn't have been more than five feet four. If he'd called her cute, though, she'd probably have pushed him into the harbour.

'Maybe I'm the one who could use the company.' He brushed off her comment. She might not want his help, but she was going to get it anyway. 'What sort of job have you got that lets you stay down here for a whole month in the summer. Are you a teacher?'

'No, I'm retired.' She laughed as he widened his eyes. 'That's not strictly true, maybe taking a belated gap year is more like it. My husband and I ran a business, and I've recently sold it on, which means I've got the time and the money to decide what I want to do next.'

'What sort of business were you in?'

'Um, you know, just a... catering firm.' Her hesitation was obvious, but he wasn't going to push her for more information; if she wanted to tell him, she would.

'With that sort of background, I'm sure you're going to love the market here and there's a fantastic farmers' market on Fridays, too.' He reeled off the patter he knew by heart, the sort of information that was plastered all over the Dorton's Adventure Centre website; after all, even adrenaline junkies had to eat, and it was the centre's growing reputation for great food and high-end accommodation that was helping to set it apart from other similar centres dotted all over the country. Port Kara was attracting its share of high profile celebrity holiday makers too, and rumour had it that some of the younger members of the royal family had stayed for a few days surfing at the start of the season. Everyone was upping their game as a result, and Elliott wasn't about to be left behind.

'It'll make a change to cook for pleasure instead of for demanding customers.' Lexie smiled as she spoke.

'Catering is a high pressure business. I always admire couples who can work together in an environment like that and not want to kill each other by the end of the week.' He hoped he wasn't overstepping the mark; the last thing he wanted to do was upset her by mentioning her husband again, but he was genuinely interested. His parents hadn't been able to live together in the end, let alone work together. Their bitter divorce had taught him only too well what happened if you tried to have a relationship that wasn't your number one priority. He was more like his mother, which was something else his father told him every time he got the chance. Mary Dorton was a dreamer according to her ex-husband, but she'd poured her heart and soul into the art shop she ran in the Sussex countryside, whilst his father had been working twelve-hour days in London, and then wining and dining clients late into the evening. They'd grown so far apart that the divorce had been inevitable, but the mud-slinging and blame that had come with it could have been avoided if they'd retained the ability to see even a fraction of the other person's point of view. Now they could barely stand to be in the same county, never mind the same room.

'It was challenging at times and I'm not going to say we never argued about the business when we were at home, or brought up gripes from our home life when we were at work. And yes, there probably were times when we wanted to kill each other,' Lexie shrugged, 'but sharing a dream with the person I loved most in the world was what kept me going, even when things were at their worst and we thought we might lose everything, before the business finally took off.'

'It sounds like you had an amazing partnership.'

'We did.' For a moment they fell silent, and he wished he hadn't mentioned it, but it was too late now.

'I'm sorry, I shouldn't have asked you that.'

'Don't be silly. I came to Port Kara to feel closer to Finn and talking about him is okay if I don't focus on the accident. I know he'd have been desperate to visit the markets, if I could have dragged him out of the surf for long enough. He'd probably have told you that it was his saint-like qualities that allowed us to live and work together!'

'If you both loved it here a few years ago, I think you'll be even more impressed with how the markets have developed. There are a couple of great delis that have opened up too.'

'A foodies' heaven then? I'll have to be careful not to buy more than I can carry home.'

'Will you have anyone to cook for whilst you're staying at Myrtle Cottage? You must be expecting some visitors if you're down here for so long?' He hoped he wasn't treading on sensitive ground again.

'I'm not sure I should be telling you whether I'm planning to be in the cottage all by myself...' She put her head to one side, as if she was trying to work out his motivation for asking.

'I promise I'm not an axe murderer, and I won't tell anyone else you're out there by yourself either.' Port Kara was probably one of the safest places around, but it was still a long time for her to be on her own, cut off from the rest of the world once the tide rose up.

'I know you won't. And to answer your question, I'm not expecting anyone to come and visit. In fact, hardly anyone knows where I am.' She jerked her head back. 'I probably shouldn't say that either! It's just as well I trust you; I think saving my life puts you on that footing, don't you? I came down here to get away from everything. And if I see friends, they'll want to ask how I am all the time. Sometimes I just want to *be*. Does that sound crazy?'

'Funnily enough, I know exactly what you mean.' Lexie wasn't the only one who'd run away, but she didn't need to hear what had brought him to Port Kara. Escaping from a lifestyle he hated would sound so unimportant compared to what she'd been through. 'What about your family? They're not always so easy to shake off, are they?'

'Mum and Dad live in Portugal, and I've promised to spend a month out there when my rental of Myrtle Cottage comes to an end. It took a bit of persuading to convince them that I'll be okay on my own. And I won't be telling them anything about the little incident on the cliff, put it that way.'

'I get that, too. Parents can be... *tricky*. But I'm sure you'll find something delicious at the market, even if you're only cooking for one.' He stopped outside a large single storey building, clad with black wood that made it look like an old barn. 'This is where all the fresh fish is brought in daily. First thing in the morning you get traders turn up down here from as far away as London, bidding on stock for the restaurants up there.'

'I don't think I've ever been to a market so close to the source of its produce before.' There was a look of genuine excitement on her face.

'Shall we go inside?'

'You don't have to spend all your time with me. I think even I can take it from here, unless there's a treacherous pathway inside that I know nothing about?'

'It's perfectly safe, but I'd like to come with you, if you don't mind?' There was no reason to, she was right, but the adventure centre gave him the perfect excuse. 'My chef asked me to check whether there's been a new catch of langoustine. We've got a gala dinner tomorrow night and he needs to plan the menu.'

'When you say "your chef" does that mean you're in charge of everything at the adventure centre?'

'Yes.' He hesitated for a moment, not sure whether to tell her that the business was actually his or not. He'd seen some people's attitudes change when they realised he wasn't just the hired help, but Lexie didn't seem like she'd care either way. Fifteen years as a city trader had sucked his soul dry and the type of people who were impressed by the fact that he owned the centre were just as draining. 'I bought the adventure centre when I stopped working in London. I wanted a professional chef to run the restaurant, so we could offer our guests food that was as wonderful as the setting. Only I hadn't banked on quite how temperamental the chef I appointed would be. Any treacherous coastal path you might find would still be easier to navigate than negotiating with Carmelo.'

'Ah, yes, I've met plenty of chefs like that over the years.'

'Did you do the cooking yourself for your business?'

'Sometimes I cooked, but quite often I was the assistant chef; I suppose you'd call me a sous chef if you wanted to use the correct term, but all of us worked as a team and desserts were probably my speciality.'

'So your husband did most of the cooking?'

'He was the driving force and he'd have been in his element in a place like this.' She stopped to look at some lobsters sitting on a bed of ice on one of the stalls. 'It's hard to look at anything food related and not think about what Finn's opinion would have been.'

They wandered between the stalls in easy silence, Elliott enjoying the opportunity to watch Lexie interacting with the stallholders. Whatever her role in the business had been, she was a good negotiator, haggling for prices, and clearly more than capable of telling the best produce from anything of not quite such good quality.

'Elliott!' There was only person who shouted his name in quite that way, demanding instant attention – Carmelo. The fact that his chef had taken it upon himself to head down to the fish market to find him wasn't a good sign. He only ever did that sort of thing when there was a problem at the restaurant, and he'd made it quite clear that purchasing the produce was beneath him. He was an artist – he'd told Elliott as much – there to create, not to haggle over the price of the daily catch.

'What are you doing here? I thought you trusted Sara to take care of all of the ordering now?' Elliott had a horrible feeling he knew what was coming.

'Greg told me you here, and Sara gone. She walk out the restaurant and say she don't want to work with me no more!' Carmelo threw up his hands, as if the sous chef's disappearance had absolutely nothing to do with him.

'Do I need to ask why?'

'I just talking to one of the waitresses, Darcy. Sara go crazy for no reason.' Carmelo was doing his best to look like the wounded party.

'*Talking*?' Elliott shook his head; if Carmelo's track record was anything to go by, he'd have moved far more quickly with the young waitress than that. Poor Sara, she'd had no idea Carmelo valued her even less as a girlfriend than as a sous chef. Elliott was going to have to put his foot down this time, though, they couldn't afford to keep losing staff at the rate they were. Carmelo had already cost him a really good bar manager, who'd also had her heart broken, and the services of a cleaning company. They'd run out of options in a place like Port Kara if Carmelo didn't slow down.

'Sara take life too serious.' Carmelo gave a dismissive shrug. 'But I can't do everything!'

'Maybe you should have thought of that.' Elliott wasn't going to have it out with him in the market, especially not in front of Lexie. But when they got back to the centre, he'd be straight with Carmelo. Artist or not, he couldn't keep treating people the way he did, not whilst he was working for Elliott anyway.

'How you sort it?' Carmelo's cropped English was no doubt part of his charm when he was telling women he met that they were the most beautiful he'd ever seen. But right now, it was getting on Elliott's nerves, especially as it made it sound like he was ordering Elliott to sort something out.

'Where do you expect me to magic up a replacement sous chef from, without any warning?' Elliott struggled to keep his tone level, but Carmelo had already lost interest, his gaze drifting towards where Lexie stood quietly by Elliott's side.

'Use an agency.' Carmelo didn't even look at him, he was too busy looking Lexie up and down in a very obvious way.

'It's the busiest time of the year and everyone who's in catering, and who's good at their job, will already be employed. We'll be lucky to get anyone at all, let alone anyone as good at their job as Sara.' Elliott's jaw muscles tightened; Carmelo was still staring at Lexie, and he had a sudden urge to land a punch square on his chef's nose. 'Will you at least look at me while I'm trying to sort out the mess that you've made? Yet again.'

'Relax, I just see something so beautiful it make it difficult to concentrate. Women like Sara can be replaced, but others, they different.' Carmelo looked briefly at Elliott, before fixing his gaze firmly back on Lexie. Did anyone really fall for that sort of rubbish? Judging by the look on Lexie's face she wasn't impressed – a mixture of amusement and irritation seemed to sum it up. Either way, Elliott had had enough.

'I didn't want to do this here, Carmelo, but seeing as you don't seem to be able to take anything seriously, I'm telling you now that this is serious. If you can't stop mixing your personal life with your professional life, and rein in your outbursts, then I'm going to be asking you to follow Sara's lead and leave.' Elliott was vaguely aware that the activity around them seemed to have stopped. Shoppers and stall holders alike, all wanting to listen to the drama unfolding in front of them. The urge to punch Carmelo wasn't lessened by the smirk that had appeared on his face.

'You can't do without me. You all talk!' He'd got his chef's attention at least; Carmelo had finally dragged his eyes away from Lexie.

'Oh, I think I'd manage just fine.' He was on a roll now. Months of having to manage Carmelo's histrionics had strained their relationship, but there was more to it than that – Lexie deserved respect, she'd been through enough. The other women his chef had set his sights on did too and, whatever Carmelo might think, Sara was too much of an asset to lose.

'You seriously think you manage without me?' The chef's derisory laugh set the seal on it. It was madness when the adventure centre was full of guests, and it was the height of the season, but Elliott wasn't backing down.

'I think we'll manage much better without you. Maybe I can even persuade Sara to come back and take over from you.' He was more or less banking on it.

'Ha, she nowhere near as good as me and you get everything you deserve!' Carmelo drew back a fist and his hand shot forward, but Elliott was far too fast for him. Grabbing the chef's wrist, he twisted his arm behind his back, almost lifting him off his feet in the process.

'And so will you, Carmelo. Now I want you to go back and pack up your stuff and be gone before I get back to the centre.' Elliott kept hold of the other man, even as Carmelo tried to make another move to lash out at him, this time with his foot. 'And if you try anything else, I've got a market full of witnesses here who'll testify that you tried to hit me, and a centre full of staff who'll back me up on your behaviour.'

'You deserve to fail and *you will!*' Carmelo wrenched himself free, as Elliott finally released his grip. 'I do much better elsewhere.'

'Good luck with that.' Elliott couldn't see the expression on his former chef's face, as he turned away and marched out of the market, but he'd bet he was looking far less sure of himself than when he'd walked in.

'Well that certainly made the market more exciting than I was expecting.' Lexie grinned, and some of the tension left Elliott's shoulders. Whatever problems it caused, he was well shot of Carmelo.

'I'm sorry, I didn't mean for you to get caught in the middle of that, but he had it coming. He can't keep treating people as if they're just there for his entertainment, or as a verbal punch-bag when things aren't going his way.'

'Don't worry, like I said, I'm not as fragile as you seem to think I am; I've dealt with my fair share of temperamental staff over the years and, for what it's worth, I think you did the right thing.'

'I don't suppose you know any decent chefs who might be on the lookout for a job?' Even if he could persuade Sara to come back and take on the role of head chef, he'd still need to find her a sous chef, and fast.

'I don't know, I could ask around.' She looked at him thoughtfully for a moment. 'But if you're really desperate, I could fill in for a week or two, just until you can get some more cover.'

'You'd do that, really?'

'Uh-huh, but maybe don't ask me again, in case I realise how crazy it is and change my mind.' She wrinkled her nose. 'I just figured, as you saved me and Albie last night, it's the least I could do.'

'That would be amazing, thank you so much. This is a real imposition, but do you think you might be able to start today? I'll try ringing Sara in a minute, but we're fully booked this week, so I'm going to need you both.'

'I'll have to bring Albie.'

'Of course and if there's anything else you need, just say the word.'

'Maybe just to get my head read.' She laughed again.

'You won't regret it, I promise.' Working at the adventure centre could be the perfect distraction for Lexie, he just had to hope he could keep his foot out of his mouth for long enough not to send her running back to the peace of Myrtle Cottage before he found a replacement chef.

3

By the time Lexie got back to pick up Albie from where Greg and the others were still drinking coffee on the harbour-side, she was already regretting the offer she'd made to Elliott. She'd rented Myrtle Cottage for a stress-free summer, and now she was going to spend at least the next week or two in a sweltering kitchen, cooking for city types who had more money than sense. They must do, if they wanted to spend their spare time hanging off the side of cliffs, or potholing in the network of narrow tunnels that even some of the smugglers had chosen to avoid. Maybe that was what the fortune teller had been talking about when she'd warned her not to rush into anything. Lexie shook her head, dismissing the thought; that was ridiculous, the older woman had just been saying whatever she hoped might persuade Lexie to part with some money and have a reading. But she couldn't help wishing she'd taken a moment to think about it before opening her big mouth and making the offer. She owed Elliott, though, and whatever she did to repay him for rescuing Albie would never be enough. She'd just have to suck it up and get on with it. It would be over before she knew it.

Elliott had been on the phone the whole time they'd been

walking back to pick up Albie. First to the centre, to warn them that Carmelo was on the way and that they needed to keep an eye on him. Then to Sara, desperately trying to talk her into coming back to work, now that her ex was out of the picture.

As soon as they collected Albie, they were going straight to the centre and Lexie would be cooking lunch for thirty people, with or without Sara's help. That bit didn't worry her, it was the thought of being back in a restaurant kitchen, surrounded by other people, with their own emotions and problems, that made it feel as though her heart was beating in her head. When Finn died, she'd attempted to bury herself in work, thinking it would help. But when one of the team members had lost his temper about a missed order of oyster mushrooms, she'd had the mother of all meltdowns, in front of half the staff and within earshot of a packed restaurant. She'd thrown a frying pan against the wall, narrowly missing taking out one of the commis chefs with it. The fury had taken her breath away. How could anyone think having the wrong type of mushroom mattered when Finn was gone? Didn't they realise that *nothing* mattered any more?

She'd walked out the moment the frying pan had clattered onto the tiled floor and she hadn't stopped until she'd reached the heath, collapsing into a sobbing heap, which made even the friendliest dog walkers keep a wide berth. That was when she'd realised she couldn't do it any more. She couldn't deal with other people's petty problems, when her heart had been ripped in two. Within days the restaurant was on the market, and she'd stayed in the background until a buyer was finally found. Dealing with the finances and marketing was something she could manage. It was just people she struggled with, when the only person she really wanted was gone for good.

'Thank God for that.' Elliott blew out his cheeks. 'Sara has agreed to come back, but she's eighty miles away at her mum's place already, so she's not going to make it back in time for the lunch service. We've got a packed schedule of activities this afternoon, so we'll need to have everyone fed by two at the latest, and we usually start serving at half past twelve. But I've asked the bar manager to put up a notice to say we won't be serving lunch until one today.'

'What are you like at chopping veg and taking instructions?' Lexie looked at him. If he wanted a solution to the mess he was in, then he was going to have to get his hands dirty.

'I'm probably better at the first than the second. But, right now, I'm more than willing to accept the advice of an expert.'

'It'll be more like orders than advice; we're going to be up against it.' Lexie ran her hand over Albie's soft head. It had been her go-to form of stress relief for months, and she was going to need him more than ever now. 'How many other staff have you got in the kitchen?'

'There are three commis chefs, who work on a part time rota basis. Then there are my favourites, Pat and Vyvyan. They're sisters who've lived in Port Kara their whole lives and seem to know everything and everyone. They come in to do the washing up or a bit of waitressing, but we have to keep them apart or no work would ever get done! They're not due in today, though. So with Sara and Carmelo gone, there's just one of the young commis chefs, Billy, in the kitchen at the moment. He was almost hyperventilating when I spoke to him, especially when I told him that Carmelo was on the way back to pick up his stuff.'

'Poor kid.' Lexie ran a hand through her hair. 'Well if it's just me and Billy, I'm definitely going to need your help.'

'No problem. I'll get one of the other guides to get everything ready for my activities this afternoon.'

'What have you got planned?' Lexie looked across at Greg, who was already rounding up the rest of the diving party and heading back to the minibus, which was emblazoned with the Dorton's

Adventure Centre logo. It was parked to the left of a row of beach huts, about fifty feet from where they were standing.

'We're coasteering.' Elliott smiled at the look of confusion that must have crossed her face. 'Sorry, the terminology has become like second nature to me. Coasteering is exploring the coastline using a combination of climbing and swimming. We take the clients up through some of the old smugglers' caves and then they get another adrenaline fix by swimming through some of the rapids and whirlpools that the cliff formations create. For those who want to, we finish it off with some cliff jumps into the sea, but not everyone wants to go through with that.'

'I can see why.' Lexie shivered. When Albie had been scrabbling on the edge of the cliff, the sea below him had looked like one big whirlpool. Why anyone would want to jump from a cliff out of choice, she'd never know. But Finn would have loved it, and he would almost certainly have got on with Elliott too.

'It's far less scary than the thought of facing thirty guests with very high expectations, wanting their lunch.'

'You stick to what you do best and I'll stick to what I do best. How's that for a deal?' If Elliott tried to coerce her into joining in with his activities, that would definitely be a deal breaker, but he was nodding his head.

'Absolutely.' He gestured towards the Land Rover parked behind the minibus, which was also emblazoned with the Dorton's Adventure Centre logo. 'Shall we put Albie in my car and head up? The clock's ticking.'

'I guess we better had, unless you think we can pass off some slices of cheese, piled next to a piece of toast, as the latest deconstructed must eat?'

'Nothing wrong with cheese on toast, but at the prices we're charging, I think they might expect a bit more.'

'We'd better make sure we give them their money's worth, then.'

Following him to the car, Lexie was already running through recipes in her head. Elliott had told her they'd had some Cornish cod delivered earlier. So as long as Carmelo hadn't got to it, and slung it in the nearest dumpster, it should be pretty easy to pull something together that would meet the guests' expectations.

Elliott turned and smiled at her as he reached the car, and an uncomfortable feeling settled in her stomach. She was worrying unnecessarily though. This was simply her way of repaying the debt she owed Elliott, and in a couple of weeks it would just be her and Albie, hanging out together back at the cottage. In the meantime, what could possibly go wrong?

* * *

'You're not as bad at this as you said you'd be.' Lexie looked across from plating up the last portion of baked Cornish cod in caramelised honey, as Elliott chopped up strawberries to accompany the dark chocolate Chantilly she'd made for dessert. Having tasted both dishes, he could say, hand on heart, that they were far better than anything Carmelo had made.

'It must have been all those years in the boy scouts, getting our dinner ready for the camp fire!' He winked, wishing he'd actually been a boy scout. It was just as well he was on chopping duty, as he had less skill than an eleven-year-old in a cooking lesson compared to Lexie. For the first time he understood what Carmelo had meant, when he described himself as an artist. Watching her turn simple ingredients into some of the most delicious dishes he'd ever tasted, as well as whipping up a spaghetti pomodoro for the guests who didn't like fish, was nothing short of miraculous. She was so calm; there was none of the drama there'd been with Carmelo, and she was really patient with Billy, too, even though he'd stuttered like a school boy for the first forty-five minutes.

'You'd better get a move on with that veg.' Lexie grinned again. 'Because there's a big pile of washing up and Billy can't do all of that as well.'

Carmelo had done what damage he could when he'd turned up to collect his stuff. Billy had guarded the kitchen, with the help of Jonathan, the new bar manager, to stop him sabotaging any of the stock. But he'd still managed to phone Pat and Vyvyan, the two sisters who were the stalwarts of the centre and who'd retired from their full time jobs a few years before, to tell them they were being replaced by a couple of kids on work experience, because the centre was too tight to pay a proper wage.

When Elliott had rung them to see if they could come in and help out with lunch, now that they were down a staff member, Vyvyan had burst into tears. It had taken him ten minutes to calm her down and get the full story from her, but he'd managed to sort it out in the end. Trouble was, she'd been so upset by what Carmelo had said that she was in no fit state to come into work, and her sister had gone out. Lexie had just shrugged and said they'd manage somehow, and he liked her all the more because of it.

'Billy's been brilliant, don't you think?' Elliott stopped chopping again, as Lexie took the first tray of desserts out of the fridge.

'He's great, he really listens, and I can see the passion in his eyes when he's working with the food. I think he's got the potential to be really good, with the right training. Where did you find him?'

'All the commis chefs are studying catering part time and working here the rest of the time, but I think you're right, Billy has got the most potential.' Elliott had sent him out to the bar to get himself an iced drink. Billy had worked non-stop, doing everything Lexie asked him to, and getting through as much of the clearing up in between as he possibly could. He deserved a quick break, and, for a few minutes, Elliott and Lexie had the kitchen to themselves. 'Have you trained chefs before?'

'I don't mind you asking me questions, as long as you keep chopping!' Lexie was like a different person when she laughed. 'But, yes, I've been involved with training a few chefs and I can already see that Billy's got what it takes.'

'This catering business of yours obviously wasn't a burrito stall, or a burger van on the side of the motorway, was it?'

'Not exactly, although I had one of the best meals of my life from a burrito stall at a street market in California.' Lexie had an uncanny knack of changing the subject, when he got too close to finding out more about her. 'Do you think Albie's okay?'

'Jonathan got one of the bar staff to take him out for a walk earlier, but I'm sure he's been making himself at home on my sofas.' They'd put the dog in Elliott's apartment as soon as they got back to the centre, and he'd heaved himself straight up onto one of the sofas, in front of the floor to ceiling windows that looked out onto the sea. When they'd left he'd been barking at the seagull sitting brazenly on the balcony outside.

'I like the fact that you didn't shout at him to get off straight away. Anyone who's nice to Albie automatically goes up in my estimation.'

'Why don't you go and check up on him when Billy gets back? I think we can cope with garnishing the Chantilly.'

'Are you sure?'

'Absolutely. You've more than earned half an hour off. Let me just do the first one before you go and you can let me know if I've got it right.' Elliott fanned some slices of strawberry onto the plate, next to the pot of Chantilly, and drizzled some strawberry jus and cream next to it.

'You just need to swirl the jus a bit more artistically.' Lexie put her hand over his, moving it so that it made a far nicer pattern as he squeezed the bottle.

'I think I've got it from here.' He turned away from her as the young commis chef came back into the kitchen. 'But I'm sure Billy can give me a bit of advice if I need it. Go and check on Albie and see if he's got rid of that seagull. I'll pop up before I take my clients out coasteering.'

'I'll see you later then.' Lexie stopped and gave Billy a quick hug. 'And well done you, you've been an absolute superstar.'

'Lexie's amazing, isn't she?' Billy had gone bright red again as Lexie walked out of the kitchen, but this time it had nothing to do with the heat.

'Yeah, she's great.' Elliott concentrated on plating up the Chantilly. There was a lot he and Billy could learn from Lexie, but neither of them could afford to get too used to having her around.

* * *

'How did the Chantilly go down?' Lexie had her hand resting on Albie's head and she looked up at Elliott as he walked back into the apartment. It was weird being in a virtual stranger's flat, sitting on his sofa with her dog as if she owned the place.

'There were lots of compliments for the chef.' Elliott sat down on the other side of Albie. 'Do you think you could bear to do it again tonight, and stick around until I can get someone else in?'

'I enjoyed it, actually. Maybe getting back to work, somewhere different, was what I needed.' She could have stretched out on the sofa and fallen asleep, given half a chance, but at least the exhaustion stopped her mind from whirring for a while.

'I'll pay you, of course. Carmelo was on fifty pounds an hour, if that sounds fair? I know it's not London rates.'

'I don't need you to pay me, but you can donate whatever you think is fair to the lifeboat station.' Lexie ran her hand over Albie's soft head again. 'I'd rather they benefitted. Someone in a situation like Finn's might need them one day. And if I can help them be there when they're needed, even a little bit, then I'll happily stay on for as long as you need someone.'

'Whatever you want me to do with the money is fine by me, but I volunteer with the lifeboat crew, so I know how grateful they are for all the donations they can get.' Elliott rubbed Albie's ear and the dog thumped his tail against the sofa. The seagull that had been taunting him all afternoon reappeared on the balcony, strutting like Mick Jagger crossing a stage. Suddenly it pecked at the glass, and Albie shot off the sofa and ran straight into the window pane, hitting it with a thud.

'Are you okay, buddy?' Elliott was on his feet before Lexie, and he rubbed the dog's head gently. 'I don't think he's done himself any harm, but maybe I should pull the blind down so the seagull doesn't keep provoking him.'

'Thank you.' Lexie patted her leg and the dog trotted over. 'And I don't just mean for looking after Albie.'

'I'm the one who should be thanking you, after everything you've done today.'

'Let's just agree to be thankful that Albie's antics brought us together on that coastal path, shall we? Someone obviously realised we could help each other out.'

'Billy's got this theory you're actually undercover from one of those reality shows, like Gordon Ramsay or something, and you've been sent in to revolutionise the restaurant at the adventure centre.'

'If only my life was that exciting.' For a second she'd been tempted to tell him a bit more about the business she'd run with Finn, but if he Googled the details he'd find out things that she definitely wanted to keep to herself. It was like pulling the blind down on Albie's tormentor – some things were best kept firmly behind a barrier.

4

The smell of fresh bread was making Lexie's stomach rumble by the time she stepped outside the bakery in Port Kara. Her plan was to make the most of a day off from the adventure centre. She'd been up early and taken Albie for a long walk on the beach, so he was happy to be left behind at the cottage, stretched out on the window seat, where he could bark at the ginger cat that had started sneaking into the garden. Between the cat and the local seagull population, Albie never had the chance to get bored. She was planning to join him on the window seat when she got back and read a few more chapters of the book she'd barely managed to get through a page of since starting in the restaurant.

'Lexie!' Billy was calling her name from the other side of the street and she waved in response. He was with a woman, who Lexie recognised as his girlfriend from the photos he'd shown her. Crossing the road to meet them, she smiled.

'You must be Aisha? Billy talks about you all the time.'

'Not *all* the time.' Billy's cheeks flushed as they so often did, but Aisha squeezed his hand.

'That's actually a relief, because he talks about you a lot too.

Apparently you're a genius.' Aisha grinned; she clearly wasn't the jealous sort. 'And having tasted the key lime pie you made when he brought some home, I have to say I agree.'

'Ah, you're both too kind. So where are you off to today?'

'We're going to the Rock Oyster festival in Wadebridge.' Billy said. 'You could come with us if you fancy it? There's all kinds of food, music and art displays there, plus of course more than enough local oysters to feed half of Cornwall.'

'That sounds fab, but I couldn't leave Albie for that long.'

'You can bring dogs, if that's all that's stopping you?' Aisha could see through her excuse.

'You've got me; I have a date with a freshly baked loaf, half a pound of mature cheddar, a bottle of red and a good book.'

'Sounds pretty great to me.' Billy looked over Lexie's shoulder. 'Although you'd better have a water-tight excuse at the ready for why you can't make any other plans this afternoon, because Pat and Vyvyan are headed this way and they're looking pretty determined.'

Pat and Vyvyan were the two sisters in their sixties who worked in the restaurant on a casual basis, coming in to help with the washing up or do a bit of waitressing whenever they were needed. Vyvyan always had her hair piled on top of her head, secured with diamante hairpins, and Pat had a business-like bob that was countered by the bright red shade of henna hair dye she seemed to favour. They'd been trying to persuade Lexie to meet some of the other locals since she'd started at the centre and she was running out of reasons why she couldn't take them up on their offer. Somehow she doubted whether they'd be as willing to leave her to her lazy afternoon as Billy and Aisha had been.

'Ah the lovebirds!' Vyvyan pinched Billy's cheek with one hand and Aisha's with the other. She was like the great aunt everyone seemed to have, who'd spit on a hanky to wipe your face clean. Billy and Aisha should be grateful for small mercies.

'We didn't expect to see you in town, Lexie, did we Vyvyan?' Pat looked at her sister for confirmation. 'I thought you said you'd be busy all weekend, with friends down from London.'

'Ah yes, unfortunately they had to cancel at the last minute.' Lexie hated lying to them, but being honest and saying she'd rather keep herself to herself outside of work would probably have hurt their feelings. It wasn't that she didn't like the sisters, she did, but getting too attached to Port Kara, and the people who lived there, wasn't going to do her any favours when she moved on at the end of the summer. She still had no idea what she was going to do now that she'd sold the restaurant she'd run with Finn, but she wouldn't find the answer in Port Kara. It was just a stepping stone along the way.

'Well, what a shame for them, but brilliant for us!' Vyvyan beamed at her. 'It means we'll be able to take you out for lunch now.'

'I've just been and stocked up at the bakers; I was going to head home for a quiet afternoon and catch up on some reading.'

'We can't have that!' The look on Pat's face echoed her words. 'We've been trying from the moment we met you to find a time that you were free for us to show you the real Port Kara, and here you are suddenly at a loose end. It's too good an opportunity to miss.'

'And what about you two?' Vyvyan turned to Billy and Aisha. 'Can we interest you in joining us?'

'Oh we'd have loved that, but we're off to the Rock Oyster Festival.' Billy sounded genuinely regretful and Lexie felt a pang of guilt. The whole team at the Adventure Centre had been so welcoming to her, with the exception of Sara, Carmelo's ex-girlfriend and the other chef, who'd been a bit prickly from the start. Pat and Vyvyan were just trying to make her feel like part of the team, and the least she could do was grab a quick lunch with them. Albie would be more than happy snoozing in the sun until she got home, and there'd be plenty of time to take him for another long walk before the tide came in.

'Maybe we can arrange to all get together another day?' Lexie said and Vyvyan's sigh was audible. She was obviously expecting her to make another excuse and put off the lunch date until Billy and Aisha could make it too. 'But I'd love to come to lunch with the two of you today, if you're sure I won't be gate-crashing?'

'Of course you won't, it'll be great.' Pat clapped her hands together. 'And Morwenna will be excited to meet you too, we've told her all about you.'

'Who's Morwenna?' Lexie was pretty certain they hadn't mentioned the name before. Vyvyan was a widow, and as far as she knew Pat had never been married, but she knew for certain that neither of them had any children.

'She's our cousin; we're having lunch at her place.' Vyvyan had already threaded her arm through Lexie's, as if anticipating that she might try to escape.

'I can't just turn up unannounced at your cousin's house. It would be so rude.'

'Don't you give it a thought, my love.' Vyvyan tightened her grip. 'She'll probably know you're coming before we even get there.'

'What do you mean?' Lexie was starting to regret accepting their invitation already.

'You'll see.' Pat nodded at Billy and Aisha. 'You lovebirds have a good time, we've got things we can show Lexie in Port Kara, but some of them she needs to find out for herself.'

'See you later and good luck.' Billy had an unreadable expression on his face and she wasn't sure she even wanted to know what the *good luck* comment meant. Although she had a horrible feeling it was one of the things she was about to find out for herself.

* * *

Lexie held on to the slim hope that they'd be going into one of the bistros in the Victorian arches, when they headed in that direction. It was where she'd been accosted by the fortune teller the day after she'd met Elliott, and she breathed a sigh of relief when there was a closed sign on the door of *Trelawney's Fortunes* as they stopped outside. So much for Morwenna knowing she was coming, she obviously hadn't even remembered the lunch date with her cousins.

'Oh what a shame. It looks like we might have to reschedule.' Lexie turned to Vyvyan, who still hadn't loosened her grip.

'Nonsense, she's closed up so we can have her all to ourselves.' Vyvyan pulled her forward and Pat was already knocking on the door of the shop.

'Come in, come in.' Morwenna pulled back the door, ushering them in without missing a beat when she spotted Lexie. Whether she'd been aware that her cousins would be bringing a guest or not, she certainly had a welcoming smile. She was wearing another headscarf, this one was covered in yin and yang symbols, and she smelt of vanilla. As Morwenna shut the large wooden door behind them, Lexie was caught by surprise; the inside of the shop was nothing like she'd imagined. It was painted in muted tones and there were lots of mirrors, and shabby chic wooden signs with life affirming messages about believing in yourself and following your dreams. There was a whole wall filled with books and DVDs and not a crystal ball in sight.

'It's not what I expected in here at all. It's nice.' The words were out of Lexie's mouth before she could stop them, but Morwenna didn't look the least bit offended.

'What *did* you expect?' She smiled in Lexie's direction and there was no choice but to be honest, even if the scene she was about to describe drew on every possible stereotype imaginable.

'I don't know, maybe a crystal ball, or a wall mural depicting the signs of the zodiac and a velvet covered table, with a deck of tarot cards.' The heat rose up Lexie's face, even before the other three women started to laugh.

'Oh no my love, I'm not a fortune teller, I don't believe in all of that nonsense!' Morwenna dropped an expert wink.

'But it says *Trelawney's Fortunes* outside and you tried to tell me my fortune the day after I arrived in Port Kara. Do you remember me?'

'Of course I do.' Morwenna tilted her head to one side. 'But I wasn't telling your fortune, I was just trying to give you a bit of advice. I recognise a broken heart because I've had one, and I made a lot of mistakes trying to outrun my feelings. I was just hoping I could make you stop and think, so you didn't do the same. It was downright nosey of me, but I can't help myself I'm afraid.'

'But then you said your cousin would know I was coming with you before we even arrived.' Lexie turned to Vyvyan, still trying to work out what was going on. 'I thought you meant that she was a psychic or something, or at least pretending to be.'

'Well yes, but only because almost everyone in Port Kara is as nosey as the Trelawneys are. When we walked past the florists, if Paulette saw us she'd be straight on the phone to Morwenna telling her that we were heading in her direction with the new girl from the restaurant. Everyone's on high alert for celebrity spotting these days, but it doesn't stop them talking about the locals' comings and goings just as much as they always have.'

'So if the shop isn't a fortune tellers, what do you do?'

'Why don't you come in and sit down and we'll tell you all about it over lunch.' Morwenna gestured to another door at the far end of the room.

Following Vyvyan and Pat through the door, Lexie was greeted by another surprise. There was a round scrubbed-pine table, laden with food and pots of chrysanthemums and hydrangeas on every other surface.

'This is incredible.'

'I'm glad you like it.' Morwenna pulled out a chair, indicating that Lexie should take a seat. 'The chrysanthemums symbolise hope and optimism, and the hydrangeas are for gratitude and understanding.'

'They're certainly beautiful.' Lexie wasn't sure what else to say. She didn't believe in flowers bringing about understanding, any more than she'd have believed that Morwenna could read her fortune by staring into a crystal ball. 'I'm so sorry I didn't bring anything with me, but I had no idea I'd be taking advantage of your hospitality today. You're more than welcome to this fresh loaf I got from the bakers, though. I'm afraid it's all I've got.'

'There's no need for that; I always have enough to feed a small army when I invite my cousins over. Now tuck in my love or you'll lose out. As you can see they don't stand on ceremony for anyone.' Morwenna laughed as Pat and Vyvyan proved her point, piling their plates high with seeded rolls, cold meats, cheeses, and salad as colourful as a rainbow. If the salad tasted half as good as it looked, she'd have to ask Morwenna what was in it, so she could try and replicate it at the restaurant.

'Now tell me, Vyvyan, have you still got your eye on that Jory from the butchers?' Morwenna looked at her cousin, who dipped her head. She was usually outspoken and the first to dish out gossip, so it was surprising to see her looking so coy.

'Of course she does. She's been mooning over him for five years now. On and off.' Pat wrinkled her nose. 'She's always in that blessed shop and we've enough pork chops stocked up in our deep freezer to start our own pig farm, if you could only master a resurrection spell Mor. Or maybe just brew up a love potion so that Jory takes leave of his senses and finally asks Vyv out on a date.'

'You do spells?' The skin on the back of Lexie's neck prickled. What on earth had she got herself into? Suddenly she wasn't sure she wanted to drink what Morwenna had poured into her glass, which she'd assumed until that point had been cloudy lemonade. She might not believe in fortune telling, but she clearly believed that plants could influence emotions. So maybe Morwenna was more of a witch...

'Of course she doesn't; Pat's joking!' Vyvyan gave her a nudge. 'It's just that my sister thinks the whole thing is a big joke too. It's not that easy at my time of life, asking a man if he'd like to take me out for a drink.'

'When you first started loitering outside the window of the butchers, like a dog salivating over a string of sausages, you were barely out of your fifties. What was your excuse then?' Pat gave her a knowing look.

'A salivating dog? Hark at you painting such a romantic picture.' Vyvyan gave her another nudge. 'You should give that Mills and Boon a ring and let them know what they're missing out on from a wordsmith like you. No wonder you've had about as much romance in your life as a doorknob.'

'That's your trouble all over though, Vyvyan. You're sitting around waiting for poor old Jory to stagger down the high street, in that white butchers' coat of his that he can barely button up these days, and carry you off *An Officer and a Gentleman* style. He's had at least one knee replacement that I know of and his lumbago's legendary around these parts.'

'Are they always like this?' Lexie couldn't help laughing at the expression on Morwenna's face.

'They have been since we were all knee high to a grasshopper, but they tell me they're on their best behaviour when they're up at the restaurant?'

'They aren't usually in the same place at the same time. If Vyvyan's on washing up, then Pat will be helping out with the waitressing and vice versa. Elliott told me when I first started there that it worked out better that way and now I know why.' She looked briefly in the sisters' direction. They were still baiting each other and they didn't seem to have noticed that Lexie and Morwenna had stopped listening to them.

'Ah yes, Elliott. Now there's a man who could scoop you into his arms and carry you off like Richard Gere did to Debra Winger, but I bet you've never even seen that film have you? You're far too young.'

'I hate to admit that I haven't.'

'And is Elliott seeing anyone?' Morwenna fixed her with a look, and she knew what was coming. Pat and Vyvyan had dropped a dozen or so unsubtle hints about what a catch Elliott was within half an hour of being introduced to Lexie, and now it looked like their cousin was about to do the same.

'Not as far as I know, but I could try putting a good word in for you if you're interested?' She kept a straight face, even as Morwenna's mouth started to twitch with amusement.

'If I was ten years younger.' She grinned again. 'All right, thirty at least; I might even have been willing to give that love potion Pat is on about a try.'

'I thought you didn't believe in all of that.'

'I don't, but I do believe in the power of positive thinking. If someone believes that something is going to help them, even an inanimate object like a potted plant, then they can harness the thing that really can help them. Their own mind.'

'I see.' Lexie wasn't sure she saw at all, it still sounded like a load of nonsense to her.

'You think I'm barmy, don't you?'

'Not barmy, just...' She was struggling to find the words. 'I'm not into all that visualisation sort of stuff.'

'Different things work for different people. But tell me this, why do you think people read their horoscopes?'

'I don't know, to kill a bit of time?' Lexie shrugged. 'Or I suppose to read something into the prediction that fits what they're hoping for?'

'Exactly. If someone reads in their horoscope that they'll meet the person they've been waiting for in the next year, or they'll get the promotion they've been after, it gives them hope right?' Morwenna shrugged. 'So maybe the astrologer's a phoney, writing whatever things pop into his head to fill column inches in the local paper. But even if he is, if that makes someone believe they can achieve their dream promotion and strive all the harder for it as a result, then surely that's a good thing?'

'I just think it's all a bit hippy dippy. I prefer to live in the real world; all this spiritualism just seems like one fad after the other to me.'

'You might be right but it can't do any harm to try, especially if the real world isn't living up to someone's expectations.' Morwenna laughed again. 'At least it doesn't do any harm for me, it's how I make my living. But I suppose I'd describe myself as a life coach if I had to put a label on it.'

'Do you hold classes or something?' Lexie had tried all of that after Finn died: counselling, life coaching, meditation and mindfulness classes, to help her learn to live in the now. All it had done was make her long all the more for the past, but it seemed to work for some people, and good on Morwenna if she felt she could help. At least she wasn't asking anyone to cross her palm with silver.

'I do some classes, and I write and sell affirmations and paint them on bits of driftwood I find on the beach. I sell self-help books and crystals, some of the books have mantras and some even contain spells of a sort. Not the eye of newt and toe of frog stuff, you understand, more chants and instructions on how to light candles to help bring about visualisations of what you really want. Some of the books are far more down to earth and describe practical steps to achieve the life you want. There's something for everyone in my shop. I even grow and sell potted plants and advise people to fill their houses with the flowers that are meaningful for what they want to achieve. That's why I call the place *Trelawney's Fortunes*. We're each masters of our own fortune and believing that is the greatest gift a person can possess.'

'I wish it was that easy.' Lexie whispered the words, and Vyvyan and Pat finally looked over at her. She didn't know how much of her conversation with Morwenna they'd caught, but she knew why they'd brought her here; they wanted to fix her. If putting a couple of crystals on her windowsill, or hooking a sign that read '*She Believed She Could and She Did*' over her bedpost would mend what was broken, then she'd have emptied Morwenna's shop in a heartbeat. But some things couldn't be fixed.

'I didn't know when I saw you that first day what had happened to your husband – Vyvyan told me last week – but I recognised the look in your eyes. I lost a baby when I was about your age and my husband walked out with all our savings – and the local barmaid – six months later, when he couldn't understand why I wouldn't just move on.' Morwenna sighed. 'You had that same look I saw in the mirror every day for months afterwards. I know there are some things you wish you could change that no amount of positivity can deliver. But you can be happy again, I promise.'

Lexie didn't say anything, and Vyvyan reached out and touched her hand. 'I hope you didn't mind me telling Mor about what happened to your husband, sweetheart? It just broke our hearts to see the look on your face when you told us, and I thought she might be able to help'.

'That's just the thing, no one can help me with that and there's nothing that any of us can do to bring him back.' Lexie didn't pull her hand away. They meant well, but none of them had any idea how she felt, not even Morwenna. She was right, they'd both been through a tragedy, but that didn't make them the same.

'Can you just answer me one thing?' Morwenna's lilting tones were gentler than ever. 'You can't bring your husband back, but if you could have the answer to one question, what would it be?'

'What am I supposed to do now?' It was the same question she'd screamed into the darkness of their bedroom night after night, in the weeks and months after he'd died. She'd sold the business, not because she'd made a conscious decision that it was the right thing to do, but because she couldn't bear to be there without Finn. She hadn't so much as made a choice, she'd simply realised she didn't have one. Now she had nothing to focus on. There'd be no work to throw herself into once her time filling in for Elliott was over, and she just wanted someone to tell her what she should do.

'There's an old Cornish saying our Granny was fond of: *them as has marbles can play and them as don't has to watch on.*' Morwenna looked at Lexie as if what she'd said was supposed to make sense, but she didn't have a clue what she was supposed to take from that. 'What I mean by that is even though you've lost your husband, you're still here and you've got so much to live for. Some people don't have the choice, they've got nothing, but you've still got a pocket full of marbles and a whole world of options. So you should start playing the game again now and stop standing around just watching. The longer you do that, the harder you'll find it to ever join in again.'

'If you mean I'm supposed to find someone else, then I'm not ready to do anything like that.' Lexie folded her arms across her chest. She'd lost count of the people, over the past couple of years, who seemed to think that was the answer to everything. There were the well-meaning stories from family and friends, about widows and widowers who'd met the loves of their lives within months of losing their spouses. But even worse than that were the people who'd actually tried to fix her up with single friends they had, as if

Finn could be replaced by her neighbour Abbie's colleague, Dave from accounting.

'She's not talking about relationships, are you Mor?' Pat didn't wait for a response. 'She's talking about you grabbing life by the short and curlies.'

'I might not have put it quite like that, but Pat's right.' Morwenna stood up and took a package wrapped in brown paper and tied with string from the shelf behind her. 'This book really helped me when I was trying to get myself back on track. It might not be the thing that works for you, but it could just help you work out the answer to your question about what comes next. Don't open it now, take it home and look at it when your mind is open enough to explore the answers that only you can really hold.'

'Thank you.' Lexie shoved the package in her bag, next to the loaf of bread, not sure if she'd ever open it. Maybe she'd just stick the book on the shelf in the cottage and leave it for someone who was looking for all that sort of self-help mumbo jumbo. Working in Elliott's restaurant for a couple of weeks was her best chance of finding out what she wanted to do next. She hadn't been able to stand being in their old place without Finn, but maybe if she bought somewhere new – somewhere that memories of him didn't fill every corner – she could find a way to make a living from doing what she loved again. If she could be happy working in the kitchen at the adventure centre, then maybe she could be happy in a new restaurant of her own, too.

Pat and Vyvyan might not have helped in quite the way they'd hoped by bringing her to Morwenna's, but at least the conversation had focussed her mind. By the time she left Port Kara in September, she was determined to have a plan for the next phase of her life. And, for the first time in a long time, she felt a tiny frisson of excitement at what might lie ahead, instead of sheer terror at doing it all without Finn.

5

Lexie's first two weeks working at the adventure centre passed in a blur. She was splitting most of the cooking duties with Sara, so she'd been able to have a lie in on Sunday morning, before heading up to the centre in time to help out with Sunday lunch, when both she and Sara would be working together. Usually, they took turns to cook breakfast, then one of them led the lunch service and one of them the evening, with the commis chefs splitting the shifts between them. Although they also took a whole day of service each one day per week, so that the other could take the day off. There'd been a few occasions when they'd needed to work together, too. There were the gala dinners on Friday nights, and the farewell lunch on Sundays, just before the guests checked out, and there was a brief hiatus until the next group of guests checked in on Monday morning. It meant the centre was always empty on Sunday evenings, and Lexie suspected it was the only time Elliott took off.

Walking up to the centre with Albie in tow, she spotted Elliott coming back with a group of guests in one of the minibuses, the roof stacked high with surfboards. Finn was never far from her thoughts, and just catching a glimpse of a surfboard could hit her like a physical blow to the stomach. But, when she was working, whole chunks of time passed when he wasn't at the forefront of her mind. She'd even woken on the morning of the last gala dinner thinking about what she needed to prepare, rather than Finn being constantly on her mind from the moment she opened her eyes. It wasn't until she got up and let Albie out, spotting a surfer already riding the waves in the distance, that it had hit her all over again.

'Sorry, darling.' She'd said the words out loud and Albie had turned to look at her, thinking she was talking to him, as she so often did these days. Finn might not be able to hear her, but she'd wanted to apologise anyway. How could she be pushing his loss further down the list? Grabbing her mobile phone, she'd scrolled through the pictures of him from their last trip to Cornwall, trying to remember what his laugh had sounded like and the feel of his arms around her. She couldn't let her memory of him start to fade, it was all she had left.

'What's for lunch today, then?' Elliott called out and raised his hand, bringing her back to the present.

'The main course is up to Sara. I'm just the assistant chef today.' Lexie gestured towards the dog, who was already pulling on his lead. 'I'm just going to put Albie up in the apartment, if that's okay? I think he's keen to get settled in his favourite spot.'

'No problem. I've made sure all my favourite shoes are safely locked away!' Elliott grinned and Albie wagged his tail in response, as if he knew he was the topic of conversation. In the first week Lexie had worked at the centre, Albie had done something he hadn't done since he was a puppy, and chewed up one of Elliott's Gucci loafers. Elliott didn't miss a beat, though, dismissing the over seven hundred pounds pair of shoes as ridiculously impractical for his life down in Cornwall. Instead, he'd gone out and spent nearly as much on toys and other bits for Albie, including a slow-release ball filled with treats, and a doggy sofa that was probably more comfortable than the lumpy one the rental company had put in Myrtle Cottage. No wonder Albie was trying to drag her towards Elliott, he was the dog's new favourite person.

'I still think you should be serving cream with that. Seems pointless to make home-made sorbet, when I bet nearly everyone would rather have cream to take off the tartness of the pie.' Sara was standing so close to Lexie that, if she'd taken a step backwards, she could have stood on her toes. And there were times during the course of preparing the Sunday lunch together that Lexie had been sorely tempted. She wasn't going to argue with Sara, but she wasn't going to be a doormat either.

'The sorbet is quite sweet and I've always found it has a lightness that can lift the tart. But if anyone wants cream instead, I'll make sure the servers know to say it's available.' Lexie had prepared most of the desserts the day before, including the sorbet, which had been frozen overnight, so she just had the plating up to supervise. She'd been assistant chef to Sara during the main course, and literally bitten her lip a few times to stop herself commenting on the way Sara spoke to Billy. She'd been tempted to suggest some ideas for preparing the main course with a bit more imagination, too, but since she was leaving as soon as Elliott found a replacement, there was no point risking really upsetting Sara, and leaving him with the task of finding two new chefs, instead of one.

'Carmelo would never have done it that way.' Sara sniffed. 'But he had a magician's touch when it came to combining flavours, so I suppose you can't expect to live up to that.'

'I wouldn't try.' Lexie forced a brightness into her voice that she didn't feel. 'I know you miss Carmelo, but I won't be here for much longer and, with any luck, Elliott will manage to find a new chef who has a similar magic touch.'

'It won't be the same.' Sara sighed and Lexie caught Vyvyan's eye. Pat was working, too, helping out waiting the tables to cover for one of the waitresses, otherwise she might have given it to Sara straight. As it was, Vyvyan decided to wade in with her opinion, neither one of them able to hold back when they had something they wanted to get off their chests.

'I don't know why you keep harping on about Carmelo, my love, he treated you worse than a dog most of the time.'

'You wouldn't understand, Vyvyan.' Sara's tone was sharp. 'I had a connection with Carmelo that went beyond what most people can comprehend. If waitresses like Darcy throw themselves at him, then that's hardly his fault, is it? He's got an aura.'

Lexie had to press her lips together to stop herself from laughing; this was even more spiritual mumbo jumbo than Morwenna peddled in her shop. It was difficult to believe that Sara wasn't joking, especially as she'd made Elliott promise that there was no chance of Carmelo being reinstated before she'd agreed to return. In less than two weeks she seemed to have had a complete change of heart about her ex.

'He did, my darling; trouble was, he was willing to share his aura with almost anyone!' Vyvyan laughed and Lexie concentrated on slicing up one of the pecan pies she'd made, to go with the hazelnut cream, so that she didn't catch Vyvyan's eye again. She wouldn't be able to hold the laughter in if she did. Placing the first row of desserts on the kitchen line, where the servers picked up the food, they were whipped away by Pat almost as soon as she'd set them down. It was time for a change of subject.

'Come on then, Vyvyan, surely you or Pat must have heard who's put an offer in on the beach house at Figgy Bay?'

'I certainly have, my love, and you're never going to guess who it is!'

'Please tell me it's a young, good looking millionairess, whose only desire is to find a penniless commis chef to settle down with. I'm sure Aisha would understand, me selling my body is the only way we'll ever save up for a deposit on a house.' Billy grinned. He'd kept quiet when Sara was in full flow, and was plating up the desserts with Lexie, but he was only too willing to join in with Vyvyan's guessing game. He and Lexie had fallen into an easy way of working, which meant she didn't have to give him instructions all the time. She was going to miss him when Elliott managed to replace her.

'No chance! I'm just hoping the new owner has a secret thing for slightly older women, if the rumours are true.' Vyvyan put the palm of her hand up to her forehead and pretended to swoon.

'Are you going to come out with it, or just stand there wasting more time when you should be getting on with the washing-up? I know this job is just a time filler for you, but some of us take it seriously,' Sara snapped at Vyvyan, who just smiled in response.

'Now, now, don't you be getting like that with me because you can't stand the suspense. I'm just building up the excitement, that's all.' Vyvyan tapped her nose. 'Don't forget, I still remember when the biggest news in Port Kara was the lifeboat house getting a fresh coat of paint. It's only in the last few years that the great and good have started to flock here. So I'm making the most of it, while it lasts!'

'Whoever it is, they'd be lucky to bag a date with you. I just feel sorry for Jory at the butchers for missing out, if you run off with a Hollywood megastar.' Lexie grinned at Vyvyan, who blew her a kiss.

'See, this girl knows how to get me to spill my secrets.' Vyvyan waved the tea towel she was holding with a flourish that a magician would have been proud of. 'The rumour is that Jasper Holland has put in an offer on the house.'

'Really?' Sara looked the most animated Lexie had seen her all week. 'Who'd have thought we'd have an Oscar winner in our midst... I know he's nearly sixty, but I still wouldn't kick him out of bed! I read somewhere that he's a bit of an adrenaline junkie too.'

'I saw an article about that as well!' Vyvyan was virtually dancing on the spot. 'He could become one of our regulars.'

Most of the guests were residents on week-long stays, but non-residents could also book events on a day or half-day basis. And, according to Vyvyan and Pat, the centre had already catered for a number of celebrities who owned holiday homes in Port Kara.

'You don't look very excited, Lexie. Don't you know who Jasper Holland is?' Sara said his name in the slow, over-exaggerated way that someone might use to give a non-English speaker instructions.

'I've heard of him.' She shrugged, almost as eager to change the subject as when Sara was talking about Carmelo. 'Billy, can you put these plates on the line, please?'

'Yes, Chef.' Billy's response earned him another daggered look from Sara. Lexie carried on plating up the desserts as Billy moved them to the line. Vyvyan and Sara were still talking about Jasper Holland, but Lexie couldn't bring herself to pretend she was excited about his imminent arrival. If she'd told them that she'd known Jasper for years, they probably wouldn't have believed her. Even if they had, it would have led to non-stop questions, and he was a part of her life she wanted to forget – the friend who'd first encouraged Finn to start surfing, and a reminder of their old life together. The actor may just have won his first Oscar, but if Finn had never met Jasper Holland, he might still be around, and Lexie had no desire to see someone who would rake up all those feelings.

'Can I borrow you for a minute, Lexie?' Elliott's voice behind her almost made her jump. She'd been miles away, years away too, with Finn back at the forefront of her mind, where he belonged.

'Of course. I'm sure Billy can manage to plate up the last few desserts.' As she turned, Elliott's hand accidentally brushed against hers and she could sense everyone watching them. Sara had made a play for him in the first week after Carmelo had been sacked, but it had been clear to everyone that he wasn't interested and Lexie had felt sorry for her. Maybe that's why Sara's feelings about Carmelo had come back with such a vengeance – she obviously wanted someone in her life, and it wasn't going to be Elliott. 'Is there a problem?'

'The opposite, actually.' Elliott smiled. 'There are some diners who want to give their compliments to the chef, for the dessert.'

'Oh no, really?' Heat rose up Lexie's neck and, if looks could kill, she'd be lying on the kitchen floor with Sara standing over her body.

'Yes and they're insistent they want to speak to you. Apparently the lemon tart and sorbet are...' He paused for a moment. 'I think the word they used was *exquisite*.'

'I'd rather not.' Lexie pulled a face. 'It's a team effort, anyway.'

'It's just for a minute I promise. One of them is the CEO of a bank who could put an awful lot of business our way, if he leaves here with as big a smile on his face as he had when he finished up his dessert.' Elliott held her gaze and she wanted to say no, but for some reason the words wouldn't come.

'If you think it will make that big of a difference, then I'll do it. But it really should be Sara going out there, she's the head chef.' Lexie turned towards Sara, who had an expression that wouldn't have looked out of place on a fishmonger's counter. Before she could change her mind, Elliott caught hold of her hand and more or less dragged her out of the kitchen and through to the dining room.

'Hugo, this is Lexie, she's the one responsible for that dessert you've been raving about.' Elliott stopped by a table of eight guests, directing his comment at a dark-haired man sitting at the head of the table.

'The lemon tart was amazing. Elliott made sure I got to try some of the pecan pie too and, let me tell you something, I've eaten at top restaurants all over the world and had some weird and wonderful creations – even something called raspberry air – but your desserts are something else. If you're ever on the lookout for another job, I'd be willing to make you a very good offer, as executive chef at the bank's headquarters.'

'Hey, Hugo, you didn't tell me you'd try and poach my staff if I brought Lexie out here!' Elliott's tone was jokey, but the smile didn't reach his eyes in the way it usually did.

'I didn't get where I am today by being shy about going after what I want.' Hugo put an arm around the gorgeous blonde woman sitting next to him and laughed. 'How else do you think I persuaded someone like Cara to marry me?'

'It's a really great offer, but I'm not looking for anything else right now.' Lexie took the card that Hugo slid across the table anyway, and put it in her pocket. Like the one that Morwenna had handed her, it was destined for the bin, but he didn't need to know that. 'It's lovely to hear you enjoyed the desserts so much. Although it's really a team effort and there's a young commis chef out in the kitchen, who you might want to make that job offer to in a year or so.'

'If Elliott's got any sense, he won't let either of you go.'

'I'm not intending to, if I can help it.' Elliott caught her eye again and gave her an apologetic smile. She hoped it was all just for Hugo's benefit – she'd been straight with Elliott from the start that this was just a temporary arrangement.

A second later their conversation was interrupted by a loud

bang, as someone threw the doors of the restaurant open with considerable force, and Lexie turned her head just as Carmelo charged in.

'This your plan from start? You want get rid of me and move your woman in?' Carmelo had crossed the room in a few steps, shouting the words with his face just inches from Elliott's.

'This is not the place, Carmelo. If you want to talk to me, I suggest we do it in the kitchen.' Elliott's voice was eerily calm, but there was a muscle going in his cheek, and everyone on Hugo's table was blatantly staring in their direction. Thankfully, most of the other diners had already left, except for another table of guests on the far side of the restaurant, who were just being served their desserts by Pat.

'You think you still make the rules for me?' Carmelo's eyes were open so wide that white was visible all the way around the iris. Whatever Sara had seen in him, it was a mystery to Lexie.

'Maybe not, but seeing as you're in *my* restaurant, without invitation, the alternative is for me to throw you out, and then you won't get the chance to say whatever it is you came here to say.' Elliott spoke through clenched teeth and Carmelo took a step back, the realisation that his ex-boss meant what he said finally seeming to dawn on him.

'I go into kitchen because I want to, not because you say so.' Carmelo stuck out his chin like a petulant toddler, but he followed Elliott into the kitchen anyway.

'I'm sorry about that.' Lexie turned to Hugo, who was watching her with a smile on his face.

'It's not a problem and I like Elliott's style. There's only one way to deal with ex-employees like that: ruthlessly. And I think your boss has got a handle on it.' Hugo smiled.

'I hope it hasn't ruined the end of your stay.' Elliott probably wouldn't thank her for saying what she was about to say, but she did it anyway. 'I know he's hoping your bank might want to make more use of the centre in the future.'

'Even if the only thing on offer here was a repeat of your lemon tart, I'd definitely be recommending it to the Board. But this has been a great trial run for our senior management's team building events, and we've all been really impressed with Elliott, haven't we?' Hugo turned to his beautiful young wife, who nodded in response. 'Seeing how the man who literally had our lives in his hands when we abseiled down those cliffs yesterday, can handle himself, only convinces me more that this is the right place for us.'

'You won't regret it.' Lexie nodded. Now wasn't the time to tell him that nothing she made would be on the menu next time he came back. Elliott probably had someone lined up to take over already and, as soon as he'd got rid of Carmelo, she'd ask him.

* * *

Elliott didn't miss the huge smile that broke out on Sara's face as Carmelo went into the kitchen just ahead of him. At least someone was pleased to see him back.

'What exactly did you think you were going to achieve by turning up here and causing a scene in front of the guests?' Elliott was half-tempted to walk Carmelo straight through the kitchen and out of the back door. But if he didn't let him say whatever it was he'd come to say, the chances were he'd just turn up again. This had to finish today, and finish for good.

'I came to give you second chance to apologise and admit you not manage without me.'

'Unfortunately for you, we're doing better than ever without you and the kitchen has been running like clockwork.' Sara might have been shaking her head as he spoke, but however much she was willing to forgive Carmelo, Elliott was having none of it.

'You not give me a choice.' Carmelo pulled an envelope out of his pocket and threw it onto one of the stainless steel kitchen counters. 'This just one copy of the photographs. If I don't get job back, then the internet discover what really happen here.'

Elliott picked up the envelope, just as Lexie came into the kitchen, with Pat close behind her. It was almost a staff meeting now but, as he slipped the first photograph out of the envelope, he couldn't help wondering how many of his supposedly loyal staff had been in on it. 'Do you actually think this reflects well on you as a chef?'

'By the time it all over internet, I go home to Spain.' Carmelo ripped the envelope out of Elliott's hand, sending the contents fluttering all over the kitchen work station. There were photographs of Carmelo, opening boxes from a well-known food wholesaler, which was famous for supplying chain restaurants with ready-made and frozen desserts. In each of the photographs, Carmelo was also displaying a menu from the centre's restaurant, with the claim that the desserts about to be served were all made on the premises.

'And are you all in on this?' Elliott looked straight at Sara, who shook her head.

'Darcy help me take the photographs.' Carmelo was still leering, like he had something to be proud of. 'She help me in lots of other ways!'

'How could you!' Sara grabbed one of the photographs and started ripping it to shreds. 'Last night, on the phone, you kept saying you wanted to come back here for me and that Darcy meant nothing to you. But all the time the two of you were cooking up this scam together and stringing me along like an idiot, so you could find out what was happening here.'

'I think the words "cooking up" are a bit ironic in the circumstances, don't you?' Elliott still couldn't work out how much Sara knew, but judging by the look on her face, Carmelo had been lying to her all along, too.

'You hard work. Darcy easier, and not just on eye.' Carmelo's face was like stone, even as Sara started to cry.

'I don't suppose Darcy knows what you called her, does she? Just a stupid kid with a crush on you!' Sara balled up another photograph and threw it in Carmelo's face. 'But I was the stupid one, wasn't I? I took this job back because I was angry with you, but then I calmed down and I hoped I might be able to talk Elliott round into giving you your old job back. Right up until about five minutes ago, I still believed you might have meant some of those things you said to me and, even more stupidly, I still loved you. But now, on top of the lies and the cheating, you've probably cost me my job. *I hate you!*' She screamed the last words, slamming her fist against the metal surface of the work station, making the rest of the photographs fly up in the air.

'That your problem.'

'I can't... I...' Sara was crying so hard she couldn't speak. Grabbing her bag from under one of the workstations, she ran towards the back door that led out to a small courtyard, and the cliff path beyond it.

'Billy, can you go after her, please, and make sure she's okay?' Elliott looked at the younger man, who nodded his head. Even the new cliff path could be dangerous and, with Sara in the emotional state she was in, Elliott didn't want to take any chances. 'Take your phone with you and call me when you find her. You can take her home and then get yourself home, we'll manage here.'

'You think yourself hero, Elliott?' Carmelo smirked. 'Huh!'

'What I don't get is why you even took the photos? Were you always planning to blackmail me at some point?'

'I think it called *insurance*, yes? You sack me, as you threaten the other times, I have plan. Soon everyone know this place not what you say it is and then you nobody!'

'I may be nobody, but, luckily for me, I know plenty of *somebodies*.' Elliott grabbed Carmelo by the back of his jacket, twisting the fabric so it tightened around the other man's body.

'Don't Elliott, he's not worth it.' Lexie shot him a look, her eyes darting between him and Carmelo.

'You speak for yourself, my love.' Vyvyan curled her hand into a fist. 'I think Elliott should teach him some manners.'

'I'm not going to hit him.' Elliott tightened his grip on Carmelo's jacket, as he started to squirm. Hitting him might have been momentarily satisfying, but Lexie was right. 'I just want you to be clear, Carmelo, I know people in very high places – in the police and legal profession – who can make your life hell if you so much as pin one of these photographs on a noticeboard, in the sad little bedsit where you'll probably end up living. You might think this gives you something on me, but I've got a stack of invoices submitted *by you*, for all the fresh and *very expensive* ingredients you claimed to have bought for the desserts that you actually got far more cheaply from the wholesaler. They call that fraud. And, if that isn't enough to put you off, let's just say I know some people in very low places too.'

'That's more like it Elliott, you tell him!' Pat waved a tea towel in the air. Any minute, Vyvyan and Pat would start a celebratory Mexican wave.

'This is where we part company. For good.' Elliott drove Carmelo forward until they were standing by the door to the courtyard. 'Remember what I said. One whiff of you making those photos public and you'll wish you were never born. Now get out!' Opening the door, he pushed Carmelo out and slammed it so hard behind him, that some of the saucepans on the rack to the right of it crashed down onto the floor.

'Are you okay?' Lexie put a hand on his arm.

'I'm just worried about Sara. Although finding out that until you turned up, every dessert on the menu was ripping our customers off is a bit of a nightmare... I should have kept more of an eye on him.'

'How could you have known? You employed a chef so you could leave the restaurant side of things to him, not so you'd have to keep an eye on what he was doing when the kitchen was closed.' Lexie was saying all the right things, but for months his gut had told him that he should get shot of Carmelo, but he'd been too busy focussing on the rest of the business to look for another chef, and he'd let things go on for far longer than they should.

'I wondered why, when I came in early, he was always just putting the finishing touches to the desserts, you know a bit of garnish on the side or something. He took hours preparing all the main courses, and talking about what an artist he was, but looking back, I never once saw him preparing a single dessert.' Pat pulled a face.

'And what about when you asked him for that strawberry cheesecake recipe and you spent all weekend trying, and failing, to recreate it? Turns out you probably could just have gone to the frozen food aisle in the supermarket! His accent's probably phoney too, I bet he comes from Wolverhampton really!' Vyvyan started to laugh and within a couple of seconds Pat had joined in.

'You don't think he'd be stupid enough to do anything with the photos, do you?' Lexie walked back to the counter with Elliott and bent down to help him pick up the photographs and saucepans from the floor, the sisters still laughing too hard at their own joke to be of any use.

'No, he's arrogant, but he's not stupid. I meant what I said and I think he knew it.'

'So who are these people you know in high places?' Lexie handed him the last of the photos.

'Maybe one day I'll tell you.'

'And what about the people in low places?'

'I could tell you that, but then I'd have to kill you!' Elliott smiled. Everything had been easier since Lexie had arrived, even dealing with an arrogant narcissist like Carmelo. If she still wanted him to find someone else for the job, he was going to have impossible shoes to fill. And to top it all off, now it looked like he'd need to replace Sara too.

* * *

'I needed this; thanks for staying.' Elliott's face was almost entirely in shadow, except for the little bit of light cast by the table lamp on the other side of the lounge and it was dark enough to make out the lights on the boats out in the bay. Albie was lying between Lexie and Elliott's feet, snoring and occasionally flicking his back legs, as if he were running in his dreams.

'I didn't feel like cooking when I got back to Myrtle Cottage, anyway, and sometimes there are definite benefits to working in a restaurant.' After they'd finished clearing up the kitchen, and Vyvyan and Pat had set off for home, Lexie had suggested they share some of the leftovers from the Sunday lunch. It had been a long day, and when she'd offered to come up to the flat to eat with him, before heading home, he hadn't taken much persuading.

'I'm really glad you wanted to have dinner with me. I'd have been up here, going over how I should have got rid of Carmelo months ago, otherwise.'

'None of this is your fault. He abused your trust and his position, and with those references you showed me, no one could have seen this coming.'

'It makes you wonder if his former employers were trying to get rid of him, doesn't it?' Elliott topped up their wine glasses.

'Probably. I know I'd have wanted to get rid of him, if he'd worked for me.' Lexie swirled the wine around her glass. She already had a warm glow from the first glass she'd drunk, and she could happily have tucked her feet up under her on the sofa and leant against Elliott. The thought made her sit up straighter and shift slightly further away from him, as she desperately tried to conjure up an image of Finn.

'What do you think I should do about Sara?'

'She did admit to feeding Carmelo information after she came back and, even if she didn't know about him using the wholesaler, that would probably be enough to justify sacking her.' Lexie pushed her feet gently under Albie's sleeping body, before the temptation to curl up next to Elliott got too much. 'But I think you should give her a second chance. Everyone deserves that, don't they?'

'Everyone but Carmelo.' Elliott paused for a moment. 'And what about you, will you stay on for a bit longer, until I decide what to do about Sara? Or are you still desperate to get back to your holiday?'

'I'm not about to leave you in the lurch. I said I'd stay until you found a replacement for Carmelo and I will. As long as you really are looking?' She turned her head and he smiled.

'The trouble is you've set me an almost impossible task now. It was relatively easy when I was just looking for a replacement for Carmelo, but now I need to find someone to match up to you...' He reached out and touched her arm, making her body tense in response. 'I need to thank you again, by the way. Hugo left me a message to say he'd enjoyed the entertainment in the restaurant, almost as much as he'd enjoyed your dessert. He's going to be using the centre for all his management team building events for the next year, and he'll review it again after that.'

'You see, today hasn't turned out that badly after all.' She forced her gaze back down to Albie, whose snoring was steadily gaining in volume.

'None of the days since you started here have turned out badly.' She couldn't look at him. Her brain might still be 100 per cent loyal to Finn, but the wine seemed to be having far too much effect on the rest of her. 'Were you tempted by Hugo's job offer? I saw you take his card.'

'I was just doing it to be polite. Working as a corporate chef doesn't really appeal to me.'

'And it would involve going back to London. That's something I don't think I could ever contemplate.' Elliott gestured towards the window. 'Not when it would mean swapping it for a view like this.'

'That's where we differ. Much as I love it here, I can't ever really see myself leaving London permanently. A couple of times the thought has crossed my mind that I should move on somewhere new, somewhere like this, but I think London's in my blood.' Cornwall might hold happy memories of snatched weekends with Finn, but London was where he and Lexie had built their business and their home. It was where their friends were too. She might be happy to spend one summer hiding down in Cornwall from them, but sooner or later she'd have to go back.

'I hope you change your mind.' Elliott bent down and stroked Albie, who didn't even stir. 'I'll miss you both when you go.'

'He'll miss you too.' She might have been able to admit to herself that she'd miss Billy and the others, but admitting she might miss Elliott was something else altogether. 'Either way, I'd better get the old boy back home to his bed, before he starts thinking he actually lives here.'

'Let me walk you home.' Elliott was already on his feet.

'No need, he might be a lazy old thing, but Albie can spring into action if I need him.' Lexie shook her head to emphasise the point. 'And Port Kara is hardly a crime hotspot; I think we're pretty safe, especially as I can go back the beach way.' At high tide Myrtle Cottage was cut off to cars, and the only way back was down a set of stone steps cut into the cliff face, which led to a locked tunnel that ended up in the cottage's back garden. It was spooky enough in the daytime, and there was no way she'd even think of going back that way on her own at night. But being alone with Elliott suddenly seemed like a bigger risk. She was just tired, that was all, and a bit tipsy.

'Are you sure you'll be okay?'

'We'll be absolutely fine.'

'Call me old fashioned, but just for my benefit, can you text me when you get in, please, to let me know you're safe?' He unlocked the door of the flat, and she looked up at him, nodding. 'Thanks again for today.'

'Anytime.' Moving her head, just as he lowered his, her lips brushed against his for a split second.

'Oh God, Lexie, I'm sorry. I was just trying to kiss you on the cheek.'

'It's my fault, I moved my head, it was just an accident.' Her words spilled out and she was glad of the opportunity to duck her head to clip Albie's lead on, now that the dog had finally got to his feet. 'I'll see you tomorrow.'

She didn't even wait to hear his response. Morwenna had told her she'd discover the answer to what she should do next, if she opened her mind. She still wasn't sure if she could go back to working in a restaurant full time, but she was more certain than ever now of what she *didn't* want. And that was another relationship. Accidental or not, kissing Elliott had left her feeling like an even bigger fraud than Carmelo and it was a mistake she wouldn't repeat.

6

Lexie had been doing her best to avoid spending any time alone with Elliott since their accidental kiss. Although that didn't stop her feeling guilty, despite knowing Finn wouldn't have wanted her to. They'd even talked about what she should do if anything happened to him, after one of his friends was killed in a motorcycle accident, leaving his young widow behind. He'd told her he wanted her to move on and allow herself to find love again. His favourite saying had been *'you only get one life'*, it was the reason he used for never being afraid to try something new, and to explain the pure adrenaline rush he got every time he rode a wave, despite the danger that might lurk beneath. She'd told him to do the same if anything happened to her, but then she'd never been a risk taker. Unless she got into a freak accident with a No.46 bus to Hampstead, she'd be fine. Except she wasn't, she was the one who'd been left behind and that was so much harder. Finn had it easy, he didn't have to grieve, or wake up wracked with guilt that she was living life without him.

Despite feeling horrified about what had happened, Lexie had agreed to stay on at the adventure centre for a few more weeks, after Sara had refused Elliott's offer of a second chance. She was too embarrassed apparently, and had accepted a job managing a branch of a burger chain in Plymouth. There was no way Lexie could leave Elliott in the lurch and she really enjoyed working with Billy and the others, so she'd decided to stay on until he managed to replace Sara and Carmelo.

It meant working pretty long hours and it was nice to spend a rare morning off having breakfast with Pat, Vyvyan and Morwenna, to celebrate Vyvyan's sixty-fifth birthday. She would be too busy at the restaurant later to go with them for afternoon tea, or to Trenowden's wine bar for cocktails that evening, so a full English and a pot of Tetley would have to do.

'Ah, there you are, Lexie. We were beginning to wonder whether you'd decided to stand us up.' Morwenna waved her hand as she spoke. She was wearing her trademark headscarf, the latest covered in crystal balls, and Lexie wondered if she'd bought it especially for her benefit; the thought made her smile.

'If only you really were psychic, you'd have known I was on my way!' Lexie took a seat in between Vyvyan and Pat, at a table outside what had been Finn's favourite café. 'I'm sorry I'm a bit late. I decided not to bring Albie, in case he couldn't behave himself. So I wanted to take him for a decent length walk before I came over.'

'As long as you're here, that's all that matters.' Vyvyan patted her arm.

'Happy birthday to the lady of the hour.' Lexie slid a package across the table. 'It's nothing much, but I saw them and thought of you.'

'Oh, they're beautiful sweetheart.' Vyvyan beamed as she opened the box and took out one of the hairgrips, which was topped with a Celtic knot, set with diamantes. There were twelve of them, enough for Vyvyan to pile up her hair and pin it firmly in place, as she always did.

'They're fancy, Vyv; you could put them in when you pop into the butchers later and buy us another couple of chops. After all, we can't risk running out, we've only got about sixty of them left in the freezer after dinner last night.' Pat clearly wasn't going to stop teasing her sister, just because it was her birthday.

'Maybe you should just tell him it's your birthday and see if he gives you a birthday kiss.' Lexie smiled again. She'd love to see Vyvyan get what she really wanted for her birthday.

'Oh I couldn't do that. I'm waiting for him to make the first move.'

'It's been five years, Vyvyan, you'll be dead before he gets around to it at this rate.' Pat slapped shut the menu she'd been reading.

'What I don't understand is why you don't enlist Morwenna's help.' Lexie looked across at their cousin. 'You must have some idea of how Vyvyan can make things happen?'

'Oh she's tried all that.' Pat pulled a face. 'She even went to see him with some crystals stuffed down her bra last year. Fell out all over the butcher's shop floor, they did! That took some explaining didn't it, Vyv?'

'I had to say I'd been fossil hunting on the beach, and I had to forgo my pork chop shopping for the best part of a fortnight after that. I could barely look Jory in the eye!' Vyvyan was able to laugh about it now.

'I keep telling her she doesn't need all of that.' Morwenna gave Lexie an exasperated look. 'She just needs to be herself. If Vyvyan was the person we know and love when she goes into the shop to talk to Jory, he'd have asked her out years ago. But she puts on this persona and, when you're not authentic, the people that matter can't connect with you.'

'Oh my goodness, yes!' Pat was getting into her stride again. 'She puts on this posh voice, which sounds like she comes from Knightsbridge rather than Port Kara. Plus he must think she's got some weird addiction to pork chops by now.'

'I just tried to make a good impression that's all, when he first moved down here from Truro and opened the shop. It would look even weirder if I dropped the accent after all these years.' Vyvyan shook her head. 'I guess I'll just have to give up on Jory and set my sights on Jasper Holland when he moves into the house in Figgy Bay. Now there's a man it'd be worth putting chicken fillets in my bra for, never mind crystals.'

'He wouldn't know what had hit him!' Morwenna said, but Pat was quick as a flash.

'It'd be her boobs hitting his shoes if she eventually took her bra off, he'd know what had hit him then! The poor sod might never walk again.'

'You haven't forgotten it's my birthday, have you? You're supposed to be nice to me today.' Vyvyan laughed. 'At least you're looking good, Lexie, you seem to have a glow about you more and more, as each day goes past. Life in Port Kara is obviously agreeing with you.'

'She's had a Cornish summer's kiss, it's as obvious as the nose on your face.' Morwenna tilted her head to one side and Lexie felt her face go red. She couldn't know about the kiss, could she? Surely Elliott wouldn't have mentioned it, and Lexie certainly hadn't. It was just another lucky shot in the dark.

'I haven't kissed anyone.' Even to her own ears it sounded like she was protesting too much, and Morwenna raised an eyebrow. If she'd realised Lexie was lying she'd obviously decided not to blow her cover.

'Of course you haven't. In Port Kara, that's just what we call a bit of colour, a sun tan, you know? A Cornish summer's kiss is just our way of describing the sun-kissed look everyone's after when they head down here to take advantage of the weather.' Morwenna held her gaze for a moment. 'Now shall we get on and order this breakfast, before it's time for lunch?'

'That sounds like a good idea to me.' Glad of the chance to stare down at the menu, until the heat had left her cheeks, Lexie just hoped that Pat and Vyvyan hadn't seen through her too. Kissing Elliott had been an accident she wanted to forget, but if the sisters found out they'd never let it go.

The days when Lexie wasn't working seemed to last twice as long as the ones when she was. She hadn't felt any inclination to paint since Finn had died and without it she had no idea how to relax. So poor old Albie was getting fitter than he'd been in years.

'Come on, boy. Let's go for another walk.' Albie lifted his head from where it was resting on his paws, looking less than enthusiastic about the prospect of heading to the beach again. 'I know we've already been once, but it'll do us both good.'

The walls of the cottage felt like they were closing in and it was giving her too much time to think. She could have gone back on her plans and asked a friend to come down and stay, but she'd wanted the solitude to plan what to do next. The centre and the new friends she'd made were taking up most of her time but, when they didn't, the solitude was almost suffocating. She was no nearer to knowing what she wanted to do with this new life, one that didn't have Finn in it, than she had been when she'd arrived, despite Morwenna's advice. She'd even started reading the book Morwenna had given her, but if she'd been hoping for some sort of epiphany then she'd have been sadly disappointed. There were no easy answers, no matter how much the self-help books tried to convince you otherwise.

She stepped out of the cottage into a gloriously sunny Sunday afternoon; the tide was out and the beach was quite busy. There were some young families making sandcastles and digging in the golden sand, and groups of people who'd clearly come to Port Kara in the hope of doing a bit of celebrity spotting. Why else would you head to the beach wearing Louboutin heels and false eyelashes, like the three girls she passed who were perched on a picnic blanket taking selfies and giggling?

'I swear, it says on the *Spotted in Port Kara* Instagram feed that Jasper Holland is down here today, and he's supposedly throwing a big party next week. I promise you won't be sorry we came here instead of going to Ibiza, Amy. We just need to meet one of his friends and bag ourselves an invite to that party!' One of the girls, who had long red hair, so straight it looked like it had been ironed, thrust her phone towards her friends, and Lexie had to drag Albie away from them before he put big sandy footprints across their blanket.

If the rumours about Jasper were true, then she was going to have to keep a low profile. The last thing she wanted was to bump into the man she held responsible for Finn's death. He'd be happy to entertain the three giggling twenty-somethings who were so eager to hunt him down, though. So she just had to hope that Jasper would be too preoccupied to head down to the surf. If she spotted him clutching a surfboard, like he didn't have a care in the world, she wasn't sure she could be responsible for her actions.

'Hey, Lexie, I've been calling your name for about two minutes, but you didn't even look up.' Elliott was suddenly standing in front of her, wearing shorts, running shoes, and a t-shirt that clung to his torso. Lexie didn't turn around to look at the girls on the blanket again but, if she had, she was certain they'd have been staring in Elliott's direction.

'Sorry, I was a million miles away. Eavesdropping on a stranger's conversation. It looks like you're making the most of your afternoon off, though.'

'I wanted to have a run before I head down to the lifeboat station for training. I suppose it's not everyone's idea of what to do with an afternoon off, but it works for me.' Elliott reached down and patted Albie's head; the dog stared up at him with a look of utter devotion.

'How often do you train with the lifeboat crew?'

'At least once a fortnight and we've had a couple of call outs already this month, but luckily everything turned out okay on both occasions.' Elliott shrugged and Lexie couldn't help thinking again about how well he'd probably have got on with Finn. They were both risk takers, or at least Finn had been before it cost him his life.

'I think it's amazing that all of you volunteer to do that.'

'You're the talk of the lifeboat station, actually.' Elliott grinned. 'In fact, if you and Albie have got time, maybe you could walk down there with me and have a chat to some of the others? They really want to meet you.'

'Do they? Why?'

'Partly because of the money you've been donating, but mostly because of the food you've been sending down. It's made you *very* popular.'

'It's the least I can do.'

'So you'll come down, then?'

'If you really think they'll want me to? Albie and I need to stretch our legs anyway.' Lexie fell into step beside Elliott, as they continued across the sand. The lifeboat station was at the far end of Port Kara beach, on the edge of the horseshoe-shaped harbour that clung to the bottom of the cliff face on one side. Billy was now working full time in the kitchen as the sous chef during his summer break from college, and Elliott had agreed to try out other chefs from a catering agency, in the hope of finding the right person to take on the head chef's role. They were also using the agency staff to provide cover for days off and holiday leave, which left Lexie with more time to herself than she sometimes wanted. The chef who they'd trialled over the last week was okay, but okay wasn't what Elliott wanted for the centre, and neither did Lexie. She might not be staying there, but Billy would be and he deserved to work with the best. It might take a while to find the right person, but at least Elliott was doing something about it now, so he'd seemed to accept that she wouldn't be around forever.

'They'll be okay with me bringing Albie into the lifeboat station, won't they? I don't want to risk leaving him tied up outside.' Ever since Lexie had started at the centre, she'd been sending desserts down to the crew and it was nice to hear they were appreciated.

'Are you kidding, they'll love Albie. He'll probably be their mascot by the time you leave.'

'He does tend to have that effect on people.' She laughed as Albie rubbed himself against Elliott's legs. That dog knew a soft touch when he spotted one. 'What have we got coming up at the centre this week?'

'We've got a big one-day event booked in for a company called Going Dutch, and they want to throw a party at the end of the day, but they want to hold it on the beach. So we're going to be pretty busy.'

'Do you usually do that sort of thing? The logistics of hosting a catered party on the beach sounded like a nightmare to Lexie, all those memories of getting sand in her sandwiches as a child weren't easy to forget.

'If the clients want it, and they're willing to pay enough, then we'll deliver what they ask for if we can.' Elliott gave her an apologetic smile. 'I know it will give you and Billy a few challenges, but when I set up the adventure centre I wanted to do something different, and embrace everything the Cornish coast has to offer. What could be better than a beach party, after all?'

'I'll just have to make sure Albie steers clear. It's enough of a nightmare when he gets a whiff of a barbecue when we're on the beach, and he stole a doughnut off a little boy on Tuesday. I had to buy the whole family ice cream to make it up to them! That's why I'm not letting him off the lead today.

'You can't blame Albie; it's hard to resist when you see something you really want.' Elliott caught her eye for a moment. 'Although sometimes what we want isn't the best thing for us.'

'Hmm. Too many doughnuts aren't good for anyone.' She had no idea if that's what Elliott meant, or if she was reading far too much into it because she was still so embarrassed about the kiss. Either way she wanted to change the subject. 'How long have you been volunteering at the lifeboat station?'

'Ever since I moved down here last year. This is the adventure centre's first full summer season, but it was good to have a release from work whilst I was getting it all set up. It stopped me fixating on the threat of losing everything if it failed. Seeing people at their most vulnerable, when their lives could quite literally be swept away, reminded me that even if the worst happened, it wasn't that bad in comparison.'

'I didn't think risks worried you?'

'It's probably the idea that I'd live up to my father's expectations that worried me the most.'

'Don't you mean *fail* to live up to his expectations?'

'You'd think so.' Elliott didn't look at her as he spoke. 'But he fully expected me to fail, in fact he told me I would. He thinks I've thrown everything away by leaving a well-paid job in London to set up what he calls a "scout camp for grown-ups".'

'Has he ever seen what you do?'

'He wouldn't come down here if I paid him. Although he doesn't do much he isn't paid to do. He's been obsessed with money, and how to make more of it, ever since I can remember. When I was a child, he left the house every morning to head to work in the city, and got home long after I'd gone to bed. I barely knew the man, but I was desperate to make him notice me. That's why I went to work in finance like him, but I felt like it was choking the life out of me from day one.'

'I've got to admit I can't imagine you in a job like that.' Lexie's eyes slid towards him again; Elliott looked like he'd been born to scale the Cornish cliffs, rather than the corporate ladder.

'I can't either, not now. Looking back, I don't know how I did it for so long.'

'Well the centre's definitely not failing. So your dad can be proud of you.'

'I won't hold my breath. He keeps telling me just how much like my mother I am, and, as far as he's concerned, that's about as insulting as he can get.'

'I take it they aren't together any more?'

'They always lived separate lives, but when Mum finally realised her dream of opening an art gallery in Brighton, she wasn't around in the tiny pockets of time my father saw fit to make for her.' The bitterness in his voice was obvious. 'That's when he decided that only his personal assistant really understood him. Mum's happier than she's ever been, though, but she's throwing herself into making her business work and, with the centre to run, I don't get to see her much. As for my father, I haven't seen him since I left my job in London.'

'That's really sad.' It was tempting to tell him that maybe he should offer his father an olive branch. She knew better than anyone that someone could be snatched out of your life permanently without warning, and she was certain Elliott would regret it if that happened before he'd had the chance to make peace with his father. But it was none of her business and she didn't know the whole story. It would be like someone urging her to move on from her life with Finn and try something new; as Morwenna had said, Lexie was the only person who knew if and when she'd be able to do that.

'So you're the famous chef we've heard so much about?' Jonty, who headed up the lifeboat crew, shook Lexie's hand enthusiastically, and Elliott shot him a look. He'd told his friend not to say anything that would give Lexie the wrong idea about him, but it didn't look like Jonty was going to play ball.

'Hardly famous!' Lexie laughed. It was great to see her looking so carefree; she was like a different person to the one he'd met up on the cliff that first day. She'd saved the centre's reputation by stepping in to help, but he liked to think it had done something for her too. There were still moments when she had that look, the one that made it obvious her world had fallen apart, but she was definitely laughing more. Port Kara had been good for her. He hoped she'd realise that and decide to stay, but until then he tried not to think about how quickly the weeks were going past. He already found it impossible to imagine going into the kitchen at the adventure centre and not seeing her standing there.

'Put it this way, the crew scramble much more quickly for one of your desserts, than they do for a call out.' Jonty hadn't even glanced in Elliott's direction since he'd brought Lexie into the station, so his warning look had been wasted. 'We've all been wanting to meet you to thank you for donating your wages to the station, as well as for the great food. But Elliott seems keen to keep you to himself.'

'Lexie's been busy up at the centre.' Elliott was beginning to regret suggesting that she visit the lifeboat station at all. It was all very well the crew winding each other up, but he'd told Jonty how badly Lexie had been hurt, and there were some occasions when the playground banter needed reining in. 'She's probably only got time for a quick hello.'

'Rubbish! Come on in and I'll introduce you to the others, and bring Albie. We've heard loads about him too.' Jonty still didn't turn and look at Elliott as he led Lexie off. Some friend he was.

Grabbing a shower whilst Jonty was telling Lexie God knew what, Elliott tried to focus on the week ahead. When he'd spotted her on the beach, he'd wanted a reason to stop her heading in the opposite direction; visiting the lifeboat station had seemed like a good idea at the time.

'I thought you'd left.' Lexie was sitting on one of the seats outside the small galley kitchen, which faced the kit room, after he'd got changed. Albie was lying at her feet, until he saw Elliott and got up. At least one of them was still pleased to see him. Although, if Jonty had said something to upset her, she wasn't showing any signs of it.

'I needed a shower after my run. Did Jonty give you the full tour?'

'He certainly did, and he said you'd replaced these chairs and some of the kitchen equipment with the donations you've made from the centre.'

'The donations are nothing to do with me. It's money you would have earned from your shifts at the centre, if you hadn't decided to donate it.' He smiled, wishing he had time to stay and chat to her for longer. When they were at the centre, it was always so hectic, and since the accidental kiss she'd seemed cagey about being on her own with him. Usually he looked forward to the lifeboat training, but he'd rather have spent the afternoon with Lexie, assuming she'd have wanted to. There was never going to be anything between them and he didn't want that sort of complication anyway, but that didn't stop him enjoying her company.

'I don't need the money, so I'm really glad it's gone to such a good cause.' Lexie stood up. 'I'd better get on, but I didn't want to leave without saying goodbye. I don't do that any more... just in case.'

'I'm only going to training.'

'And Finn was only going surfing.' Lexie frowned and he had to clamp his arms to his side to stop himself reaching out to comfort her. It was a natural reaction, but it would probably have freaked her out.

'I'll be fine and I'll see you in the morning. I promise.'

'Just don't break that promise and let me down, okay?' She gave him a serious look.

'I won't.' Elliott swallowed hard. He couldn't begin to imagine what she'd been through, he just wished he could say something to make it easier, but sometimes words just couldn't cut it.

* * *

The lifeboat headed out to sea just as the wind began to pick up, and Lexie watched Elliott and the others disappear into the distance.

'Does he remind you of Finn? I can see the resemblance, in a way.' The voice behind her was instantly familiar but, when she turned around, she was suddenly unsure.

'Jasper?'

'Guilty as charged, but for heaven's sake keep your voice down. Keeping a low profile around here is a full time job.'

'Is the new look for a part?' She raised an eyebrow, the colour of the big bushy beard Jasper was sporting was definitely out of a bottle, and the cap pulled down low over his eyes hid the rest of his face.

'No, it's because this part of Cornwall is full of bearded, surfboarding hipsters and, like this, I blend in. There are far too many autograph hunters in Port Kara at the moment and I bought the house here to try and get away from all of that.'

'So it's true then, you bought the beach house at Figgy Bay?'

'I certainly did, but you were the last person I expected to find down here. Until I heard that you were staying at Myrtle Cottage for the summer.'

'How on earth did you—' She didn't even bother finishing the question, already knowing the answer. Jasper had connections everywhere and if he wanted to find out where someone was, he would. 'Have you been checking up on me?'

'Let's call it checking in. I owe it to Finn.'

'Well you don't owe *me* anything.'

'You still hate me, don't you?' Jasper adjusted the peak of his cap, so that he could fix her with his famous stare and she shook her head slowly.

'I don't hate you, I hate what happened to Finn, and I hate you for introducing him to a life that ended up with him dead on a beach halfway across the world.'

'Don't think I haven't thought about that myself, but Finn died doing what he loved. He was always chasing the next adrenaline high; you'd never have opened a restaurant in London if he hadn't been a risk taker, but you were the anchor he always wanted to come home to.'

'Until he didn't.' She wiped a tear away with the back of her hand, annoyed with herself for crying in front of him.

'He wouldn't want you to bury yourself down here, living a half-life. I saw the way you watched Elliott Dorton getting into the lifeboat. I've seen that look before, Lexie, and I recognise the pull between two people when I see it.'

'Oh sod off, Jasper. Your trouble is you feel a pull towards every even vaguely attractive woman you meet. Until the next one comes along, that is.'

'Harsh but true. A real connection is very rare though and I've obviously touched a nerve. The question is, are you going to act on it?'

'That would suit you down to the ground, wouldn't it? You could let go of whatever tiny thread of guilt you feel about Finn's death then.' Lexie shot him a look, annoyed that he'd brought the worst out in her so quickly. 'How the hell do you even know who he is, anyway?'

'One of the reasons I moved down here was because of his centre's growing reputation. I want to pack as much adventure into life when I'm not filming as I can. I have so many goddamn clauses in my contracts now to prevent accidents or injuries, so I don't disrupt filming and cost the studio money. When I'm not working I want to try everything I can. I had my assistant do some research on the sort of activities that were available in the local area when I saw the house in Figgy Bay, and Elliott Dorton's place is one of Port Kara's biggest selling points. I got a small private beach with the house when I bought it, but the surf on the main beach is what draws everyone here, including me. Plus, there are paparazzi constantly lurking near my place almost all the time. But even if I want to use the main beach, I have to hide behind the beard and hat, so that I look like everyone else. Although maybe not everyone... Take Elliott, for example, he's in a different league.' He paused and fixed her with his stare again. 'The real question is how do *you* know him? I never had you down as the adventurous type, even before Finn's accident.'

'He rescued Albie from a cliff edge after he ran off and we just sort of became friends.' She wasn't going to tell him about her volunteering at the adventure centre; whoever it was that he'd paid to spy on her obviously hadn't found that out. She didn't want to give Jasper any more ammunition to clear his conscience. He'd been with Finn on that fateful surfing trip, and he'd been one of the friends to perform CPR, and the first person to offer Lexie support – financially and otherwise. But when everyone, including Jasper, just carried on with their lives after the funeral, she was the one left in agony. If that had made her bitter, then she couldn't help it.

'I saw the two of you walking along the beach together when I was coming out of the surf. Even Albie seemed to approve.'

'We both like Elliott, but that's it. Just because it was easy for you to replace Finn with another surfing buddy, it doesn't mean I want to replace him. I'm not interested in a relationship.'

'Who said anything about a *relationship*?' Jasper roared with laughter, turning a few heads on the beach as he did. He lowered his voice, clearly realising he might be about to reveal himself to the dreaded autograph hunters. 'What you need is a fling. You've been drifting since Finn died and if you don't do something about it now, you could be stuck in limbo forever. We both know he wouldn't have wanted that. Instead of analysing everything and thinking that the first decision you make without him has to be perfect, just have some fun for Christ's sake. Make some mistakes, keep things casual and then you'll have more of an idea of what it is you actually want.'

'Have you been to *Trelawney's Fortunes*, down in the town by any chance, and spoken to the woman that runs the place? She's always in a headscarf.'

'Fortune tellers aren't really my sort of thing; I don't know if I'd want to hear what they have to say. In any case, I'm afraid the only locals I really notice are the ones in bikinis!'

'So not exactly a qualified relationship expert, then?'

'Okay, so I might not be a relationship expert, but I'm an old man, I know what I'm talking about.'

'You're not old. You're not even sixty yet.'

'Yes, but like Finn always said, you only get one life, and I'm making the most of mine, especially now that the years seem to be going by so quickly. Go out and grab yours and make Elliott your first mistake, or a warm memory you can look back on when you're as old as me.'

'Don't use what Finn said against me.'

'Don't get defensive when you know I'm right, then.' Jasper held up his hands. 'Look, in the end, it's up to you, but I just don't want you to be lonely.'

'I'm fine, I've got Albie and...'

'You can't finish that sentence, can you?' Jasper didn't even wait for her to answer. 'Why don't you come to the house? We can have a dinner party like we used to, in the old days. I won't even make you cook.'

'Nothing is like it was in the old days.' Lexie turned back towards Myrtle Cottage. 'I'll see you around, Jasper.' Walking away from him, she didn't turn back, even when he called out her name. All she needed was Albie, whatever Jasper thought. She just hoped she'd be able to shake off the voice in her head that was repeating Finn's favourite phrase. You only got one life and she didn't want to waste it. But Jasper was right about one thing, she was so terrified of making a mistake that she could barely decide what to have for breakfast, let alone make a decision about the rest of her life.

7

Elliott had hardly had a chance to talk to Lexie since he'd taken her to the lifeboat station, but he'd decided not to quiz her about what the other crew members had said anyway. If Jonty had made a comment that she was exactly Elliott's type, or something equally inappropriate, then it would be better not to bring it up. He didn't want to make it awkward between them. In other circumstances he could have admitted that he found her attractive and he was pretty sure she felt the same, but they couldn't have been more wrong for each other – just like his parents. Physical attraction with nothing in common was fine for a fling; Elliott had had enough of those to know it could even be a benefit. But Lexie wasn't looking for any kind of relationship, least of all a casual one.

They could always stick to the safe ground of talking about the centre, though. So two days before the big event for Going Dutch, Elliott walked into the kitchen to check on Lexie's progress with the event, and to get some feedback on how the current week's agency chef was getting on. She didn't even look up, she was so engrossed in showing Billy how to create tempered chocolate cylinders on what looked like sheets of acetate. It was one of the items on the menu for the beach party. The contact from Going Dutch had said they wanted trestle tables set up on the patch of private beach that belonged to the adventure centre. It would either be a disaster or a game changer, but with Lexie providing the menu, his money was on the latter.

'Right, I think I've got it.' Billy grinned, both of them still seemingly unaware that Elliott was there.

'Why don't you have a go then? Once we've got enough cylinders, we can start on the chocolate orange mousse filling.' Lexie turned away as Billy began spreading the chocolate over the acetate, and suddenly caught sight of Elliott.

'I didn't realise you were standing there!'

'Sorry, I just didn't want to interrupt you by saying anything.' She had a smear of chocolate on her cheek and Billy looked like he'd gone two rounds in a mud wrestling tournament.

'I think Billy can take it from here? Can't you?'

'Yes Chef!' He was already moving on to the next cylinder.

'I'm sorry, I just wanted to see how the preparations are going?' Elliott had trusted Lexie from the outset, but it was hard to leave any aspects of the business out of his control when it meant everything to him, especially after what had happened with Carmelo. Things had been going so well since Lexie had arrived, though, so they had to get the right person in to replace her.

'That's okay. Billy's doing a grand job. Sadly I can't say the same for the agency chef. He went out for his lunch break two hours ago and he hasn't come back yet. He knows how busy we are, too.'

'I take it we haven't found our new head chef yet, then?'

'I'm afraid not. I just wish we had a bit longer. If I had a few months, I could easily train Billy up to head chef level, he's got so much potential.' The young sous chef's cheeks blazed with colour as she spoke, but he was still wearing a grin like a Cheshire cat.

'I wish you had longer too. Sorry.' Elliott gave her an apologetic shrug as his phone began to ring. 'I'd better take this call.'

Pushing open the back door of the kitchen to the courtyard behind it, where Lexie had started planting up a herb garden, he answered the call from an unknown number.

'Hello, Elliott Dorton speaking.'

'Ah, so you answer your phone from unknown numbers, but not from your father?' Charles Dorton had a distinctive tone, which always made it sound like he was giving Elliott a lecture. And he usually was.

'I've been busy.'

'I left you three messages.'

'I know.'

'And I suppose you haven't had a chance to return any of those calls?'

'I was waiting for the right moment.' Elliott didn't add that there was no such thing as far as he was concerned. Speaking to his dad could always wait.

'Did you listen to the messages?'

'Not all the way through.'

'I guessed you hadn't. Otherwise you'd have called.' His father's tone was clipped; there was never any hint of affection, so what Charles said next almost knocked him off his feet. 'I've read some of the reviews for that adventure centre of yours, there was a big piece in The Guardian last week. It seems to be doing pretty well.'

'We're doing okay.'

'How much money are you making?' His father's question was far less of a surprise, it was the bottom line that never changed.

'Like I said, we're doing okay.'

'Have you spoken to your mother?'

'Not this week. Have you?' He felt a stab of guilt. Elliott and his mother were both busy, but he knew he should find more time to check in on her and make sure she was okay. Although he had no idea why his father was asking. He'd barely seemed to care when he'd been married to her, let alone now.

'I haven't spoken to her either, but you're going to have to call her after this. Chantel and I are getting married, and I want you to tell your mother.'

'You're doing what?' Elliott could try to convince himself he didn't care what his father did any more, but the idea that he was marrying his former personal assistant, who was two years younger than Elliott, when she was so clearly only after his precious money, was ridiculous. But there was worse still to come.

'She's having a baby. We got a private scan this week and it's a boy. So this is my second chance to raise a son who wants to follow in my footsteps.'

'He'll be pushing you around in a wheelchair by the time he turns eighteen.' Elliott could taste the bitterness. His father was sixty-eight, thirty-five years older than his new fiancée. But if she was just a gold digger, as Elliott suspected, then they deserved each other.

'So you'll call your mother?'

'I doubt she'll care.'

'That's the problem, though, isn't it? If either of you had ever cared what I wanted, the family would still be together and I wouldn't have to be starting again in my sixties.'

'Are you for real?'

'All I wanted was a supportive wife and a son who would follow in my footsteps.'

'I tried and so did Mum.' Elliott didn't want to listen to his father's response. 'I'll talk to her because I think she deserves to know, not because you asked me to. Goodbye.'

Ending the call he stared at the phone for a moment, fighting the urge to throw it over the kitchen garden wall and into the sea beyond.

'Are you okay?' Lexie tentatively opened the kitchen door and stepped out into the courtyard, letting it close behind her. 'I thought I heard raised voices.'

'You did. I was arguing with my father again.'

'I'm sorry, it's none of my business.' She turned back towards the door, but he reached out and gently caught hold of her wrist. He needed to talk to someone and he wanted it to be Lexie.

'I hate the fact that he can make me feel like an eight-year-old again and that I'm a constant source of disappointment, but he just has this uncanny knack of doing it every time we speak.' Elliott was still holding her wrist and she took a step towards him.

'For what it's worth, I think he's jealous. He must see this life you've built for yourself, following your passion, and wonder how he let everything he does revolve around money. Deep down I bet he misses you too.' Her voice was so gentle that he couldn't help leaning his body towards hers, and she didn't move away.

'He's got a funny way of showing it. He only rang to tell me that he's marrying the woman he left Mum for and that they're having a little boy. He couldn't wait to tell me how much he's looking forward to having a son who'll finally live up to his hopes.'

'Not realising how amazing you are is his loss.' Lexie tilted her head towards him and he gently kissed her forehead, before forcing himself to pull away again.

'You're the amazing one.'

'I—' He watched her mouth, but she'd stopped talking and, despite all the things he'd told himself about what a disaster it would be to get involved with her, he could feel her breath on his skin as he pulled her towards him again. This time it was no accident. The kiss was hesitant at first, he wanted to make sure that she wanted this as much as him, but weeks of fighting a mutual attraction passed like an electric current between them.

'I've been wanting to do that for a while.' Elliott was the first to speak as they finally pulled apart and he half expected Lexie to tell him that it was an accident, a mistake they shouldn't have made, but she didn't. She opened her mouth to answer him, just as Billy flung open the door from the kitchen, making them spring apart.

'You'll never guess who owns Going Dutch?' Billy could hardly stand still.

'If we're never going to guess, you better just tell us!' Lexie laughed and Elliott had to force himself to drag his eyes away from her to look at Billy.

'It's Jasper Holland! *Going Dutch* and *Holland*, get it?' Billy was still pacing around. 'I can't believe I'm actually cooking for an Oscar-winning actor.'

'It doesn't get much more high profile than that.' Elliott turned to Lexie, and all the colour seemed to have drained from her face. He had a horrible feeling that the realisation of what they'd done had just hit her. Whatever it was, she looked utterly miserable.

'No it doesn't, which means we'd better get on with getting the menu ready. The reviews from this could make or break the centre.' She spoke directly to Billy, not turning to look at Elliott again, and two seconds later they both disappeared back into the kitchen. She'd definitely wanted to kiss him this time. So why had she fled at the first opportunity she got?

* * *

Lexie had considered leaving Port Kara altogether when she'd heard that it was Jasper Holland who was behind the big beach party. The last thing she wanted was to bump into any more of the old crowd, the celebrities who had hung out in the restaurant she'd run with Finn. It had terrified her at first, taking on so much debt to set up the business that her husband had always had so much faith in. Then, when they'd got their first Michelin star, it had all gone crazy. They went from waiting for the phone to ring, and praying that they'd have enough bookings to fill the restaurant on a Friday and Saturday night, to having a waiting list every night of the week. Of course, if you had the right name, you could always bag a table, and the restaurant had a list of celebrity clientele that any showbiz agent would have given their right arm for. Jasper Holland had been a regular and he'd soon become fast friends with Finn, who was a natural at networking and never seemed fazed, no matter how high profile their latest celebrity diner was. Lexie had always preferred to stay behind the scenes, working in the kitchen and doing what she loved best. It was why they'd been the perfect partnership from the moment they'd met, when she was just nineteen. But everything from back then seemed superficial and pointless without Finn and she didn't want to see any of the old faces, not now.

In the end, she'd decided she wasn't going to let Jasper Holland's decisions have that much impact on her life for a second time. She was staying in Port Kara until September, as she'd planned, but she had no intention whatsoever of attending the party Jasper was throwing in person. The event had been planned as a joint stag and hen do for Jasper's godson and his fiancée, who also happened to be a distant relative of the royal family. So everybody from the adventure centre wanted to volunteer to wait tables or serve drinks at the event, including Vyvyan and Pat. Lexie had designed the menu as a very posh picnic and had done her bit by preparing all of the food in advance, alongside Billy and one of the agency chefs. Elliott was taking the hen and stag party out for a series of activities, which included the opportunity to try out paragliding, as well as the slightly less terrifying option of zorbing.

Then they'd all be returning for the picnic on the centre's private beach, as the paparazzi were apparently still camped out by the private beach at Jasper's new house.

There were more agency staff, and one of the other sous chefs who went to college with Billy, covering the evening service at the centre itself. Lexie had taken Albie for a walk up to the centre to check on their progress and make sure that everyone was okay. Deciding to walk back along the new coastal path had been a whim, and she'd barely even thought about the fact that it would take her right past the centre's private beach, where Elliott and the others would be working hard to make sure Jasper's party went off without a hitch.

She was far enough away not to be spotted, but she could see the two long picnic tables that had been set up, side by side, like something you might see at a family wedding in Italy. Jasper was sitting at the head of one of the tables and his raucous laugh carried up to Lexie, on the gentle summer breeze. If Finn had been around, he'd have been down there amongst the party goers for sure. Not because he had any particular fascination with the royal family, especially not distant cousins of the queen, but because he always liked to be at the centre of what was going on. Scanning the group on the beach, Lexie tried to see if there was anyone else she recognised, as Albie stuck his nose into a patch of reed and started to dig. She spotted Vyvyan moving between the tables with a bottle of champagne, her hair piled up on her head in the usual style.

She couldn't see Elliott at first. There were a few faces she recognised from TV and magazine covers, and some of them had been regulars at the restaurant too. But he wasn't sitting amongst the guests, even though she was sure Jasper would have invited him to. That was another difference between Finn and Elliott. They were both driven, but Elliott definitely wanted the business to take the spotlight, rather than wanting to make sure he got noticed too.

'Come on, boy, let's get going.' Lexie pulled gently on Albie's lead, to get him to lift his head out of the reeds. 'We can't stay up here all day.' She felt self-conscious, suddenly, like the only kid not invited to a birthday party, pressing their nose up against the window.

Pulling a reluctant Albie behind her, she carried on along the coastal path, to the point where there was a crossroads, giving the option of either heading down the slope to the private beach, or up across the cliff towards another path that led down to the main beach in Port Kara. Just as she reached the crossroads, she heard a scream. Glancing down, she could see what looked like half the party goers running towards the edge of the water and, at first, she assumed the screams were excitement, fuelled by too much champagne and a group decision to head into the water to carry on the fun.

'He's drowning!' A woman shouted the words, her voice high, bordering on hysterical, but no one seemed to be reacting. Looking further out, she could see a man in the waves, his arms flailing as he tried to keep his head above the water. Then she saw Elliott, running full pelt towards the sea and diving in, to the left of the crowd. He moved through the water quickly and seconds later he reached the man, whose arms didn't stop flailing, even when Elliott got to him and began swimming back to the shore. Lexie could hardly breathe, her mind racing between the present and the past. Had someone swum out to Finn like that?

'Come on, Elliott, please.' She whispered the words, her hands involuntarily moving together, as if she were saying a prayer. Dropping the lead, along with her concentration, Albie seized the opportunity to taste freedom and shot down the path towards the private beach, before she even had a second to react. Finding a tiny gap in the fence that kept the beach private, he was through it in seconds.

'Albie, no!'

Her fingers struggled to press out the code on the gate, which luckily she knew by heart. Finally through she started to chase after Albie, almost tripping as her eyes kept darting towards the group of people still standing on the edge of the water, watching Elliott's slow progress towards the shore. What was wrong with them? Why wasn't anyone helping him?

Albie was much quicker than her, and he was on the beach and thundering toward the crowd before she was even half way down. It was a miracle that he'd run past the abandoned picnic and hadn't just taken the opportunity to help himself to all that unattended food. But he was making a beeline towards the water and no amount of shouting on Lexie's part seemed to be having any impact.

She was breathless by the time her trainer-clad feet hit the sand and, looking up, she could see that Albie had gone into the water. Unlike most Labradors, he usually preferred to stick to the water's edge, but not today. Within seconds he was far enough out to start swimming and he drew level with Elliott, just as Lexie finally reached the edge of the crowd who were all still just watching.

'What's Albie doing?' Vyvyan suddenly appeared at her side.

'I don't know, I think he's trying to help, but I don't want Elliott to have to go back and rescue him too.'

'He looks like he knows what he's doing, my love. He's like one of those big hairy dogs that rescue people on mountains, you know the ones with barrels of brandy around their necks.'

'Why isn't anyone else helping?' She looked at Vyvyan who shook her head.

'Elliott told us all to stay on the beach and he can be pretty commanding when he wants to be, our boss. But they'll all be okay, Elliott will make sure of it.' Vyvyan patted her arm, but Lexie couldn't take her eyes off the water until they were all safely back on the beach.

Albie circled Elliott and the other man, who finally appeared to have stopped fighting his rescuer. But he wasn't moving at all and that seemed much worse from where Lexie was standing. Turning back to face the beach, Albie took hold of the man's shirt in his mouth and began pulling him in the same direction that Elliott was swimming, and at last the crowd started to react, just as Lexie started to wade into the sea, unable to stand it any longer.

'Get back on the beach, Lexie, it's okay.' Elliott looked up in response to the noise of the crowd, shouting the instruction to her, and she hesitated for a moment before doing as she was told.

'Look at that dog, he's saving Rory!' A woman's voice in the crowd was incredulous.

'That's Albie!' Vyvyan turned towards the crowd. 'He's my friend Lexie's dog and he's a proper hero.'

'Not just him, thank God for Elliott.' It was a man's voice this time. 'I told Rory not to go in after necking that bottle of champagne.'

'I would have given Elliott a hand.' Another man said, sounding like he was trying to convince himself as much as the crowd around him. 'But he wouldn't let me.'

'Shall we call an ambulance?' One of the other women turned towards Jasper, who'd suddenly emerged from the crowd, but he shook his head.

'Let's see how they are first.' Jasper's voice was calm and Lexie knew the score. He was trying to avoid the negative publicity, if he could. It was bad enough that he'd been associated with Finn's death, and how much of that had been plastered all over the press. Having his name linked to another near drowning was the last thing Jasper, or his agent, would want.

Lexie ran towards Elliott as he dragged the man onto the beach, Albie still pulling on his shirt.

'Is he okay?'

'He will be.' Elliott turned the man's head to one side, and water began to drain out of his mouth straight away. Suddenly he was coughing up more water, and the colour immediately seemed to come back into his face, as he took in big gasps of air. 'Keep breathing, Rory, and don't try to say anything yet.'

'Do we need an ambulance?' Jasper didn't seem to notice Lexie, as he asked the question, and Elliott nodded.

'We should get him checked over, just in case. I don't think he ever really lost consciousness, but he's swallowed quite a bit of water.'

'Any chance that just being seen by a doctor would suffice? I can get my private guy down here by helicopter in twenty minutes if needs be.'

'It might be quicker in that case. He's not a high category emergency and the ambulance almost certainly wouldn't get here that soon.' As Elliott answered, Rory sat up, almost as if to emphasise that there was no need to rush him to hospital.

'I'm fine to go back to the party.'

'No, you're not.' Elliott's tone didn't allow for an argument and Rory slowly nodded his head, lying down again. 'We'll get you up to the centre to wait for the doctor, whilst Jasper puts in the call.'

'Can we do it at my place instead? It'll help keep things low key. At least it will if we can sneak him in without the paps seeing. You'll have to try and sneak me in too, I suppose.' Jasper suddenly noticed Lexie and smiled, but she didn't respond. Had he tried to hush up his presence at Finn's death in the same way, before everything else came out?

'I'll get a couple of the lads to bring a stretcher down and we can move him up to the centre. If he seems well enough to be moved again when we get up there, I'll get one of them to drive him down to your place. If you can give your doctor a call, to make sure he can get here, I'll give the centre a ring.'

'Are you okay?' Lexie dropped down to her knees on the sand beside Elliott, as Jasper disappeared to make the call.

'I was flagging until Albie stepped in.' Elliott grinned as he checked Rory's pulse, the other man's breathing getting far less laboured with every breath.

'The pair of you scared me half to death.'

'I'm sorry.' He let go of Rory's wrist and took hold of her hand. 'That must have been hard for you, after what happened to Finn. But I'm okay and so is Albie, even Rory here is going to be all right. Although going into the water like that, with so much alcohol on board, was really stupid of him.' Rory mumbled an apology that neither of them acknowledged.

'I couldn't bear for it to happen again, that's why—' She didn't get the chance to finish the sentence and explain that there was no room in her life for another risk taker.

'My doctor's on his way; he'll be here by six at the latest.' Jasper cut her off and Elliott nodded.

'I'll give Greg a call to organise bringing the stretcher down, and I'll drive Rory to your place if he's up to it. Are you coming?' For a moment, Lexie thought Elliott was talking to her.

'I'll meet you there, if I go in from the back of the house, I've got the best chance of avoiding the paps. You'll be all right until then, won't you Rory.' Jasper ruffled the other man's hair, like he might have done to Albie.

'Can I come and see you later?' This time Elliott was definitely talking to Lexie, and she hated the fact that Jasper was watching them.

'What for?'

'I need to bring this hero a big steak to thank him for helping me get Rory in safely.' Elliott bent down and patted Albie's head.

'Okay.'

'I'll see you later then.'

'Uh-huh.' Lexie wasn't going to say any more than she had to, not all the time she could sense Jasper still watching her. As Elliott walked away to call the centre and get the other guides down onto the beach, some of the party goers started to crowd around Rory. They were even taking selfies, now that the drama was over.

'I think I'm going to have to throw a bit of a party tonight to celebrate the fact that we're all still in one piece. Back to my place once the doc's seen to Rory and as much Cristal as you can drink! That includes any of the staff from Elliott's place who might like to come along and celebrate with us.' Jasper's suggestion was greeted by a cheer from the crowd, but Lexie was already walking away from him. Pat and Vyvyan caught up with her before she got very far.

'Fancy that, him inviting all of us to go to his party. It's like a dream come true!' Vyvyan put a hand on her arm to stop her. 'Don't tell me you're missing out on an opportunity like that?'

'It's not really my sort of thing. Celebrating the fact that this time he's got away with being so irresponsible.'

'*This time*?' Pat didn't miss a thing, and she'd instantly picked up on the words that could have given the game away. She didn't want her new friends to know about her history with Jasper, so she attempted a casual shrug.

'I just mean that he strikes me as the sort who throws caution to the wind for his own entertainment. He might have got away with it this time because of Elliott, but he's clearly not going to learn from it, if he's just going to spend the night downing champagne.'

'But you don't mind if we go, do you my love? After all, I can't sit in every night for the rest of my life waiting for Jory the butcher to finally pop by and ask me out, can I?' Vyvyan gave her a look that a puppy dog would have struggled to pull off.

'Of course not. I'm relying on you two to make sure they don't get themselves into any more trouble over there tonight.' She squeezed Vyvyan's hand.

'And if we get ourselves into trouble?' Pat had a mischievous grin on her face and Lexie couldn't help laughing.

'Well that, ladies, is another matter altogether! Just so long as you have fun.' Giving them both a hug, she carried on towards Myrtle Cottage. The sisters might be more than twice her age but, unlike her, they still knew how to have fun.

* * *

It was getting dark by the time Elliott walked down the path to Myrtle Cottage, but Albie jumped up at the front window and started barking as soon as he saw him. That dog was amazing, not only did he leap into the sea to rescue drowning men, but he could also smell rump steak from nearly twenty feet away. Lexie was already at the door by the time he got to it, the soft glow of the lamp on the wall outside highlighting her silhouette.

'How was Rory?' Lexie moved slightly to one side to let him in. She'd been a bit of an enigma since that first day he'd met her on the cliff and, after what Jasper had just told him, she was all the more fascinating.

'He's fine. Jasper's doctor gave him the all-clear and, last I saw, he was lying on a chaise longue in one of the rooms at Jasper's place that overlooks the sea, being fussed over by at least three beautiful women.'

'Three beautiful women, eh? Lucky boy.'

'Most people would probably say so, but I've seen better.'

'Really?'

'Definitely.'

'If he plays his cards right, he might even get to spend some time with Vyvyan and Pat. They're going over to Jasper's tonight, for a party he's throwing to celebrate you rescuing Rory.' She looked at him levelly. 'I was half expecting you to phone and say that you couldn't make it after all, seeing as the party is more or less being thrown in your honour.'

'Those kinds of parties are not really me and I'd much rather be here anyway. Although I did speak to Jasper after I checked on Rory.' He wanted to talk to her about what Jasper had told him, but he didn't want her to clam up like she had before, when she'd been in danger of opening up about the past. 'How's Albie, has he recovered from his swim?'

'As you can see, he's fine, and I think he knows what you've got for him!' Lexie laughed as Albie continued to weave himself in and out of Elliott's legs. 'I think we ought to put him out of his misery and let him have what he wants, don't you?'

'Absolutely, he's definitely earned it. If you took him over to Jasper's place tonight, he'd be given a hero's welcome.' He'd thought that mentioning Jasper again might give her the chance to tell him she'd known the actor for years, but she just brushed over it.

'It's not really my scene either. Can I get you a drink?' Lexie took the bag of steak from him, putting some of it in Albie's bowl.

'Yes, please, that would be great, if I'm not holding you up.'

'Nope, it's just me and Albie with no plans except to watch a bit of trashy reality TV later. Same as always.'

'Why?'

'Why what?'

'Why don't you have other plans? And I don't just mean for tonight.' He looked at her for a moment. 'Jasper told me a little bit about how you two know each other.'

'I bet he did.' Lexie turned away from him and opened the door of the fridge. 'Wine or beer?'

'Beer would be good, thanks.' He could feel the tension in the air as he took the bottle from her. 'I'm sorry, the last thing I want to do is to upset you.'

'It's okay, but if you're going to hear everything, you might as well hear it from me.' Lexie took a bottle of white wine from the fridge and picked up a glass. 'Let's go through to the other room and I'll tell you all about it.'

The curtain of darkness outside the cottage seemed to have closed in at the same time as Lexie had shut the front door behind him. It was a clear night and the stars that lit up the sky outside the sitting room window reminded him yet again why he loved Port Kara so much. He'd never seen a sky that big or that clear when he'd spent all his time in London, and by the end he'd felt hemmed in there, to the point where he felt he could barely breathe. There were rows of solar lights strung across the front garden of Myrtle Cottage, trying to compete with the stars, but they had no chance.

'So what did Jasper tell you?' Lexie poured herself a glass of wine as she spoke, and he wondered how much he should say. But if they were laying their cards on the table, then it was time to be honest.

'He asked me how I felt about snagging a Michelin-starred chef to work at the adventure centre, after Pat told him it was you that catered the picnic.'

'I should have told you.'

'I'm surprised you didn't, but it's up to you what bits of your past you want to share, and who you want to share them with.' Elliott frowned. 'Although I must have looked pretty confused, as I had no idea what he was talking about. Especially when he called you Alexa Douglas-Jones.'

'That's my married name and my full first name is Alexa, but my friends have always called me Lexie, anyway. But the truth is, I didn't want to be that person and everything that's associated with her, whilst I'm down here.'

'If I had a Michelin star, I'd get a wardrobe full of t-shirts made advertising it, and wear one every day, so everyone would know how brilliant I was!' Elliott laughed, trying to ease some of the tension, but Lexie shook her head.

'No you wouldn't. The Douglas-Jones' brand was really Finn's, anyway. He got his Michelin star before me and it was what drove customers to Casa Cibo.'

'But you were the youngest chef ever to get a Michelin star. I bet Marco Pierre-White hates you for knocking him off that spot.'

'You googled me, didn't you?' Lexie pulled a face. 'I never wanted all of that notoriety, I was happiest hidden away in the kitchen, doing what I loved.'

'Nothing much has changed, has it?' He took a sip of his beer. 'So why did you tell me you were a sous chef?'

'Because to all intents and purposes I was second in command to Finn. He was the figure head, the one who was happy to hang out with the customers and make Casa Cibo more than just a place to eat. It was Finn who the celebrity clientele came to spend time with, and that's how we got to know Jasper so well.'

'And you never resented that?' Elliott decided not to mention what Jasper had said, about how keen Finn had been to become a celebrity in his own right, and the ambitions he'd had to be a TV chef. But something flickered across Lexie's eyes.

'We were a good partnership and, like I said, I wasn't interested in any of that. Jasper was the one who got Finn into adventure sport, and it was Jasper who was with him when he died. But I guess you know that if you googled me.'

'I didn't google you. Jasper told me about you being the youngest recipient of the Michelin star.'

'Right.' Lexie took a deep breath. 'Well, if you google Alexa Douglas-Jones, you'll see the whole story and you'll understand why I wanted to be plain old Lexie Turner down here. That's who I was until I met Finn, and it's who I needed to be again.'

'Do you blame Jasper?' Elliott watched Lexie's face as she

seemed to consider his question for a moment and then finally shook her head.

'No... at least not any more. I did and sometimes I have, because it's easier to pin the blame on someone and have something to lash out at, than to accept it's a freak accident that could have happened to anyone. If that's the case, then why did it have to happen to us?'

'I'm sorry—'

'I know you are. Everyone is.' She shook her head again. 'But that's not it. The accident was always going to be covered in the press, because Jasper was there and Finn had become quite well known in his own right, but then things went crazy.'

'You don't have to tell me if you don't want to. And I promise not to google it, if you don't want to tell me.' He meant it, too, and it was a promise he was determined to keep, no matter how curious he might be.

'Do you know what? I believe you, and that's exactly why I'm going to tell you.' She took another sip of wine. 'After the accident, two women came forward and said they were with Finn and Jasper in their hotel suite the night before the accident.'

'Oh God.'

'They were both underwear models, so you can imagine how that made things look. They were trying to make a name for themselves and so it seemed too good an opportunity to miss.'

'So they were lying?'

'Not exactly. They were in Jasper's suite, with him, *both of them,* but Finn wasn't there.'

'Right.'

'Do you hear that doubt in your voice? That's exactly how everyone sounded and what everyone else thought, especially after all the coverage it got in the press.'

'Sorry.' He seemed to be making a habit of saying that.

'Don't be, you didn't know Finn like I did, and I know he'd never have done that to me. Much as he liked to court the celebrity lifestyle, I was his one and only, and I never doubted that for a moment, not even after the story broke. But even if I'd had any doubts, Jasper would have set me straight. He told me the truth straight away and he even arranged it with his PR team for the two girls to sell the true story of what went on with him that night, to one of the tabloids. But by then the damage was done and mine and Finn's marriage was tainted in the eyes of everyone else. The original story still appears if you google either of our names, or look up Casa Cibo, and I wanted to leave all of that behind.'

'I can understand that. Sometimes you have to reinvent yourself to move on.' Elliott's escape from the past might not have been quite so dramatic, but he'd been every bit as keen to leave it behind him and make a fresh start.

'We're a pair, aren't we?' Lexie smiled.

'Are we?' Elliott couldn't help asking the question.

'I like you Elliott.'

'You *like* me?'

'I'm not looking for any more than that.' She topped up her glass and looked across at him. 'Jasper's opinion is not usually something I set a lot of store by, he spends so much time acting that I sometimes wonder if he knows what's real any more. But the last couple of times I've spoken to him, he actually said something that made sense.'

'And what was that?'

'He said that I needed to try a few things without worrying about the future. Not everything I do now needs to have anything to do with my long term plans. I wouldn't have accepted the job at the adventure centre if I'd had time to think about it properly, but I've really enjoyed it, and it's made me realise that it's okay to live day by day, at least for a little while.' Lexie bit her bottom lip. 'So I wondered if we should, you know, try a bit of living day by day and go out together every now and then?'

'Dating?' Elliott could tell how hard it had been for her to say everything she had, but he had to be certain he hadn't got the wrong end of the stick again.

'We're attracted to each other, I think we can both admit to that.' She smiled. 'But I'm a city girl, who'll be going home at the end of the summer, and you're a workaholic who can't bear to be out of sight of the sea. So we'd never work, even if the timing was right and we didn't have enough baggage between us to bring Heathrow to a standstill. But it could be a nice way to spend the rest of the summer. You're supposed to be the risk taker, after all.'

'I really like you too.' Something was holding Elliott back, but it was stupid to read as much into it as he was. They might go on two dates and decide that it had all been a horrible mistake, or they might have the best few weeks imaginable. Either way, he'd be able to get Lexie out of his system and move on – go back to concentrating on what really mattered, the business. 'Do you think Albie will be okay with me hanging around more often?'

'Oh, I think he likes you even more than I do.' Lexie laughed, as Albie laid his head on Elliott's knee, looking up at him with total adoration as he always did.

'Well, I guess that's decided then.' Elliott ran a hand down the dog's back. The advertising slogan on the Cornish Tourist Board's website described Port Kara as a place of endless summers. So he'd have plenty of time to spend with Lexie before summer was over and they'd probably be sick of the sight of each other by then. He was relying on it.

8

Lexie had asked Elliott not to mention to the others that they were seeing each other outside work. It was just a bit of fun, that was all. So there was no point Vyvyan and Pat getting all giddy over the prospect, or giving her the third degree after every date they went on. Meeting up with the two of them and Morwenna, for breakfast or coffee, had got a lot trickier though. She had to watch what she said every time one of them asked what she'd been up to lately. And even though she knew Morwenna didn't claim to be a psychic, she had a way of watching Lexie that sometimes made it feel as if she really could read her mind.

'What are you giggling about?' Coming back to the table after ordering cream teas for the four of them, she'd caught Pat and Morwenna in gales of laughter, but Vyvyan was looking distinctly put out.

'We're just talking about Vyvyan's trip to the GP's surgery. She gave poor old Dr Pughe more than he bargained for!' Pat was still laughing.

'I couldn't help it; I was sure he said that I should lie on the bed and I needed to strip.' Vyvyan pulled a face. 'Turns out what he said was lie on your side and expose your left hip. There I was, naked as the day I was born when he pulled back the curtain. He couldn't get out of there fast enough!'

'Can you blame the poor man!' Pat was clearly enjoying making Vyvyan recount the tale.

'Oh no, that must have been awful.' Lexie couldn't help smiling, despite her words of comfort. It was all too easy to picture the scene.

'It's her own fault for not putting her hearing aid in.' Pat furrowed her brow. 'She drives me mad at home, and Dr Pughe got a taste of what I have to put up with every day. Admittedly not the stripping, thank God, but mishearing half of what I say.'

'I just want to relax when I get in. First thing I do is take off my bra and the second is to take my hearing aid out. I forgot to put it back in before I headed to the doctor's, that's all.' Vyvyan shrugged. 'I suppose I should be used to it by now. I've had the blessed things over ten years, since before Phil died, but I still don't really like wearing them.'

'I reckon it's just an excuse so she never has to answer the phone and deal with those idiots asking if we've ever had an accident that wasn't our fault. Has she ever answered the phone to you, Mor, even once?' Pat turned to their cousin who shook her head.

'I can't say I ever recall her answering the phone. Or Phil come to that matter, it's always been you Pat.'

'You've always lived together, then, even when Vyvyan was married to Phil?' Lexie knew the sisters were close, but it was a surprise to hear that they'd never lived apart, even during Vyvyan's marriage.

'We did, it suited Phil, having two women waiting on him. It wouldn't have worked for a lot of people, but our parents had passed on by the time I got married and it just seemed to make sense for us to move into the family home with Pat.'

'Shame none of us had any kids.' Pat sighed. 'Especially you Mor, after what happened with the baby.'

'Things happen for a reason.' Morwenna paused as the waitress brought over a tray, setting the tea pot and scones down on the table in front of them. 'I'd have loved to be a mum, but then I probably wouldn't have started the business or had so much time to help other people out over the years. I think this was my destiny.'

'Be careful, or Lexie will be mistaking you for a fortune teller again!' Vyvyan gave her a nudge. 'Tell us then, if everything happens for a reason, what brought Lexie to Port Kara?'

'She needed a Cornish summer's kiss.' Morwenna gave her an appraising look. 'You can see for yourself how well she's looking on it.'

'That's true.' Pat poured out some tea. 'Her complexion was the colour of the skin on a cup of boiled milk when she got here.'

'I am here you know!' Lexie said, but as long as they didn't put two and two together and factor Elliott into the equation, she didn't really mind.

'There goes our Pat again, spouting poetry!' Vyvyan spread jam across the bottom half of her scone. 'But it's true, you've got colour in your cheeks and developed a spring in your step over these past few weeks. Like we've said before, life in Port Kara obviously agrees with you. Are you sure we can't persuade you to make it permanent? The adventure centre won't be the same without you.'

'Don't put pressure on her, Vyv. Lexie will know for herself when she's found the place where she's meant to stay.' Morwenna flicked the end of the rainbow-striped headscarf she was wearing, over her shoulder. 'Not everyone's like us and discovers the place they were born is the place they're meant to be.'

'I don't know about that so much any more, myself, as it happens.' Vyvyan spooned cream onto the top half of her scone before sandwiching them together. 'I'm not sure I can stay in Port

Kara if it means showing my face down at the doctor's surgery again.'

'It's all right.' Pat looked at her sister from over the top of her teacup. 'From what I've heard, Dr Pughe is off work and undergoing a course of intensive counselling to get over the trauma of seeing you naked. All those pork chops do something to a body that shouldn't be inflicted on the unsuspecting!'

'Pat Trelawney, if you weren't my sister, I'd shove that cream scone straight in your face.' Vyvyan managed to feign offence for all of about five seconds, before she started to laugh.

'You two are incorrigible!' Lexie shook her head.

'I know, but you'll miss us when you leave.' For once Vyvyan looked serious. 'There are worse places you could settle than Port Kara you know.'

'I know.' Lexie wasn't under any illusion that there weren't things she'd miss about Port Kara. But Morwenna was right, she'd know when she'd found the place she was meant to be. There were still more reasons to leave Port Kara than to stay; even if did mean some painful goodbyes when the time came.

Elliott couldn't really label the decision he and Lexie had made to move their friendship onto something else, but it was a relief that no one else seemed to have noticed. They'd gone into whatever this was without any expectations, so having to deal with the expectations of anyone else was something they could do without. It was hard enough to grab time together; the centre was busier than ever, and they still hadn't found a permanent member of staff to take over as head chef. His suspicion that it would be almost impossible to replace Lexie had proved correct, but Billy was making huge progress under her tutorage. As a result, Elliott felt comfortable about leaving him in charge of the kitchen, supervising some agency staff, for two days when the centre finally had less guests booked in than usual. A company that had been sending its staff on an overnight teambuilding session had gone into liquidation almost overnight, which left the centre at half occupancy. Never one to miss an opportunity, Elliott asked Lexie if she'd be up for taking a road trip to check out new local suppliers for the restaurant, to add a more authentic Cornish taste to the dishes they offered on the menu.

Lexie had said she'd come along if Albie could make the trip too, and they had plans to visit suppliers of everything from locally caught crab, to Cornish yarg, a semi-hard cheese that was wrapped in stinging nettles. Elliott had booked lunch for them in Finbar Bay, which was a quirky little town, stacked high on a hillside above the harbour where allegedly the best crab in Cornwall was brought in fresh every day. He'd wondered if Lexie would resent the fact that they were spending the time they'd managed to snatch together checking out suppliers, but she'd seemed really excited by the prospect. He had a feeling she'd have turned him down if he'd suggested a romantic break somewhere, she was still holding back so much of herself. But if he was honest, he was holding back bits of himself, too.

'If I'd known Albie was dressing up for the occasion, I'd have made more of an effort.' Elliott opened the back door of the car to let the dog jump in. Albie was wearing a red and white spotted bandana collar, his tail thumping heavily against the back of the seat, as Elliott closed the door.

'You look pretty good to me.' Lexie grinned.

'I could say the same for you.' He opened the passenger side door for her, the pale blue and white striped dress she was wearing a bit dressier than anything she wore to work.

'I didn't know if I should wear something a bit warmer; they've forecast a big storm, but we should be home by then.'

'It'll be fine, the storms here always seem to hit overnight.' Elliott closed the door and walked around to his side of the car. They weren't staying out overnight; it was another unspoken agreement between them. And for Elliott it was self-preservation.

'So where are we off to first?' Lexie turned to him as he started the car, and Albie stuck his head through the gap between their seats.

'We're going to a dairy farm about twenty miles inland. They apparently won a world cheese championship for their Cornish yarg.' Elliott pulled a face. 'I had no idea there was such a thing as a world cheese championship.'

'Then you haven't lived.' Lexie laughed as Elliott pulled onto the road that led out of Port Kara. There was no one else he'd rather have been spending a rare day out of the centre with, and the conversation flowed easily between them as they drove along the twisting country lanes that took them further inland.

A cow poked its head over a stone wall as they pulled into the farmyard at the dairy. The buildings, crafted from grey stone, were arranged in a three-sided u-shape, and the longest of the low barns had obviously been converted into a farm shop at some point. There was a big sign directing visitors to the holiday cottage complex, which was housed in more converted buildings beyond the main farmyard.

'It's lovely here.' Lexie stepped out of the car at the same time as him. 'But I think we'd better leave Alb in the car as it's so much cooler today.'

'I'll leave the windows open a bit.' Elliott lowered the glass in the back doors and locked the car. The wind was definitely starting to pick up and the sky in the distance had taken on a gun-metal grey appearance. The storm might be coming sooner than either of them expected. He tried not to think about how quickly summer was galloping past, but every time he turned over the schedule where they wrote up all of the centre's events he got a reminder.

'You must be from Dorton's Adventure Centre?' The middle-aged woman, who'd crossed the farmyard to meet them, was wearing a bottle green body warmer and a welcoming expression as she thrust out her hand towards them. 'I'm Mary Polton. Welcome to Polton Dairy Farm, home of the world championship-winning yarg.'

'Pleased to meet you.' Elliott caught Lexie's eye as he shook Mary's hand, and he tried not to laugh.

'Come in, come in, we've got lots for you to sample, so there might be a few other things you want to consider us supplying. Our clotted cream is shipped out all over the world, and we've just won an international award for our clotted cream gin, too. We'll have more gold medals than Usain Bolt at the rate we're going!'

'I feel like an under-achiever,' Elliott whispered under his breath to Lexie, as they followed Mary across the farmyard. If Lexie had been staying on at the adventure centre, they might have had a chance of winning some culinary awards. As it was, he'd just have been happy if they'd been closer to finding a half decent replacement.

Their host hadn't been exaggerating when she'd said she had lots of things for them to try. He hadn't sampled the clotted cream gin because he was driving, but to be fair to Mary Polton, everything else had lived up to the hype she'd given it. Lexie had been really enthusiastic about the dishes they could create using not just the yarg and the clotted cream, but the wild garlic, cider and honey that Polton Dairy Farm had also diversified into producing over the years.

'I was thinking that if all the suppliers have as much to offer as this, we could have some weekends where all the produce is exclusively Cornish, and really make it a speciality of the centre.' Lexie's face was shining as she spoke, and it was bittersweet to hear her say 'we' like that. She had so many ideas for the centre and so much passion about how the culinary side of the business could go. But once she'd left, Elliott had no idea if they'd be able to bring those ideas alive. He'd just have to do his best.

'That would be fantastic. A true Cornish experience is the brand I've always wanted for the adventure centre. Activities like coasteering fit so well with the location and they've always felt quintessentially Cornish to me. Having the rest of the business match with that would be perfect.'

'Do you know, I'm loving this!' Mary Polton clapped her hands together with obvious excitement. 'I only wish my Basil could be here to meet you and hear what you've got to say. You're exactly like we used to be when we were first married and had so many plans for what we wanted to do with the business. It's just brilliant to see a young couple like you two with that same enthusiasm.'

'Oh we're not—' As Elliott spoke, Lexie held out her hand to stop him, shaking her head.

'You've got an amazing business here. You must be so proud of it.' She smiled at Mary. Lexie obviously didn't want to get into a lengthy explanation about their relationship, and Elliott was happy to go with it. Whether Mary and Basil realised how lucky they were was the real question. Finding your other half, someone who has the same drive and goals, was something his parents had never achieved. He'd accepted he might not find that himself – there weren't many people who were as passionate about the outdoor life as him, or whose idea of fun was abseiling down a cliff face in a howling wind in November – but it had obviously worked for the Poltons.

'It's taken decades, but we're amazed at what we've achieved when we look back, and never in our wildest dreams did we think we'd end up as world champions!' Mary looked from Lexie to Elliott. 'So have I convinced you to use us as a regular supplier?'

'Absolutely.' Lexie and Elliott, spoke at the same time, and Mary clapped her hands together again.

'See, I knew it, the two of you are totally in sync. Just like me and Basil!'

'Let's talk terms, shall we?' Keen to avoid a conversation that might make Lexie uncomfortable, Elliott shifted the focus back to business.

Half an hour later they'd agreed that Polton Dairy Farm would be supplying the adventure centre with several different cheeses, clotted cream, two varieties of gin, cloudy cider, wild garlic and honey. Elliott had even bought some organic dog treats for Albie, which were the only type they sold in the farm shop. They were gluten free, according to Mary, but he doubted Lexie's dog would even notice, Albie usually swallowed things more or less whole.

'They had some amazing produce, didn't they?' Elliott said, turning to look at Lexie as they pulled out of the farmyard. As expected, Albie had made short work of his treats and he'd get the chance to stretch his legs and go for walk on the beach, when they got to Finbar Bay.

'Yes, they've built up a brilliant business there. I'd love to do something like that.' There was a slight hint of regret in her voice. There was nothing stopping her though, she could do what she liked, and go wherever she wanted, once her holiday lease in Port Kara was up.

'You won't open another restaurant then?'

'I don't think so; I need to do something different. It won't be the same without Finn, and the restaurant was always more his dream than mine. Seeing the Poltons' business, I remembered how much I loved sourcing the produce and creating a taste that's truly authentic. At the restaurant, we tended to run with whatever was on trend, but I love what Mary and Basil are doing.'

'Cornwall would be a great place for you to run a business like that. I know you love London, but surely you can see how much potential there is down here?'

'Maybe.' Lexie sighed. 'Thanks for not putting Mary right about us not being married, by the way.'

'No problem.' Elliott hesitated, wondering whether to ask the obvious question. But he needed to know. 'Can I ask why you didn't want to tell her?'

'Because then I'd probably end up explaining that I was widowed and what had happened to Finn. Sometimes I just don't want to be *that* person. For half an hour, I just wanted to be who Mary thought I was – an excited business owner, with a million plans for how you and I can grow the adventure centre into something we can be incredibly proud of. I was playing pretend, I suppose.'

'I get it.' Elliott took the road towards Finbar Bay and they fell silent, both of them lost in their thoughts. He wanted to ask her if she thought it was something she'd always have to pretend, but that would have taken them onto really dangerous ground. Asking that would probably have had Lexie packing up her stuff and heading back to London before the week was out. And if it didn't make her do that, what then? Was there any chance that people as different as he and Lexie clearly were could ever outlast the summer? All the evidence seemed stacked against it and, like she'd said, sometimes it was easier to say nothing at all.

* * *

The Cornish scenery blurred past the car window, as Elliott drove them towards Finbar Bay. What surprised Lexie was that there were never any awkward silences between them. They could chat about anything and everything, but they could sit in silence too, without feeling the need to fill the gaps with mindless chatter, and he seemed to know when to give her space to think. Guilt was nagging at her again, in the now familiar way it did, when she let herself drift too far away from her old life. Letting Mary Polton think she was someone else, anyone but the widow of Finn Douglas-Jones, was a slight on her husband's memory. But she hadn't been honest with Elliott when she'd said it was because she didn't want to be seen as the poor young widow, at least not entirely. For a moment she'd wanted to believe that Mary's assumption about her and Elliott could be real. In another life, she could imagine them building a future together just like the Poltons, but no one got that lucky twice.

Lexie finally broke the silence. 'What's so special about the crab at Finbar Bay then? I thought the fish market at Port Kara was good enough to meet the centre's every need?'

'It's supposed to be the best crab in all of Cornwall and there are certain boats which will only sell their catch out of Finbar Bay. We're really lucky to have the fish market on the harbour in Port Kara, but I just wanted to see if Finbar Bay lives up to its promise. It was an excuse to take you out to lunch too.'

'You don't need an excuse to take me out to lunch.'

'Maybe not an excuse, but just a good reason to make the time. With things as busy as they are at the centre, both of us sloping off for lunch for no good reason might have raised a few suspicions.'

'Do you think I'm being silly about all this cloak and dagger stuff?' Lexie watched Elliott as she spoke, and he shook his head.

'No I get it.' He negotiated a hair pin bend, keeping his eyes firmly fixed on the road. 'Finbar Bay's just over the hill ahead, but you can see the harbour if you look to your right now.'

Lexie turned her head and caught a glimpse of the sea between the twin hills, that the road cut a path through the middle of. There were boats bobbing in the harbour and she could just see the top of the church spire.

'There are so many beautiful places down here. How did you decide on Port Kara?' It was her turn to question him. If Elliott hadn't told her about his past, she could easily have believed he was Port Kara born and bred. He was so at home there, and he seemed to know every inch of the cliff face and coastal path that led down from the centre to the beach.

'It found me. I looked at lots of places that had the potential to be run as an adventure centre, I even looked at a place just outside Finbar Bay, but Port Kara just felt right. The cliffs there are dramatic and challenging for climbing, and the surf is perfect. The network of caves that were used for smuggling were also a big selling point, but most of all I just felt at home from the moment I pulled up in my car. Why did you take so many holidays in Port Kara? I'm guessing you must have felt its pull, too?'

'Finn loved the surfing, and I used to paint a lot back then, the seascapes were perfect. But, like you, I just felt at home there. Running the restaurant was stressful and I remember feeling like a weight had been lifted, every time I saw the *Welcome to Port Kara* signpost when we drove into the village. And, of course, Albie loves it too.'

'Don't you paint any more?'

'No, I haven't felt like it since I lost Finn. I tried a few times, but I couldn't seem to finish anything. I was planning to do some painting whilst I was down here this time, but working at the centre hasn't left me much time.'

'I'm sorry.' Elliott's tone was gentle.

'I'm not. The truth is I don't know what I would have done with myself if I hadn't had the adventure centre to go to. It's reminded me of my first love, too. Cooking has always been my passion and my escape, but I even lost the motivation to do that after Finn died. I was going through the motions, but I wasn't feeling it. Having to step in at the centre made me throw myself back into it wholeheartedly and I'm the happiest I've been for a long time.'

'Since Finn died?' Elliott turned to look at her as he brought the car to a halt in a small car park opposite the harbour in Finbar Bay.

'Yes.' Once again, she wasn't telling him the whole truth. There'd been times in the last year or so of Finn's life when she'd wondered if they were drifting apart. Before that they'd headed to Port Kara whenever they had time off together, but in that last year, if she was really honest with herself, there'd been times when Finn had chosen to spend his free time doing other things. There'd been a couple of trips with Jasper, one to go sky-diving in the Nevada desert, and another trip scuba-diving in Israel. He'd even managed a weekend skiing black runs in Val D'Isere. Lexie had stayed at home with Albie, to run the restaurant. She'd taken her holidays separately, when Finn was back at the restaurant, flying over to her parents' place in Portugal or going to visit friends. She wasn't lonely, but that wasn't the point. She couldn't help wondering what would happen if they ever had children, but she hadn't wanted to give up on them either. They'd both worked long hours to get the business up and running, and, once it became such a big success, she could understand Finn's desire to make the most of the opportunities that had come his way. She'd told herself that they'd work through it and come out the other side, but now she wasn't sure that they ever would have done. It was why she was so happy at the centre – happier than she'd been for at least a year before Finn's death. But she didn't want to admit that to Elliott, or to herself. She'd loved Finn, she really had, but his death had put him on a pedestal and things hadn't been as perfect as she'd wanted to remember them. It was only since she'd arrived in Port Kara that she allowed herself to see that, but she still couldn't admit it to anyone else.

'I checked with the restaurant and they're happy for us to take Albie in, even if it rains.' Elliott said, as they got out of the car. 'The sky's looking a bit threatening.'

'I love a good storm, especially the electrical sort, where the lightning illuminates the sky. Although maybe not in this dress.'

'Let's get to the restaurant then.' Elliott got Albie out of the back and they headed along the path that ran parallel with the harbour. Even the air smelt of salt, and the rising wind made the dog unusually skittish.

'I hope Albie calms down a bit by the time we get to the restaurant. He hasn't been like this since he was a baby.' Lexie's hand brushed against Elliott's as she drew level with him, whilst he kept a firm hold of Albie's lead with the other hand. Curling her fingers around his, she slipped her hand inside Elliott's. They were taking things slowly, but outside of the fishbowl that Port Kara could often seem, it felt good to walk hand-in-hand.

'He'll be fine. I think he's just reacting to the wind.' Elliott laughed as Albie started chasing his tail. 'And if they don't want him in the restaurant, they'll have to do without me too.'

'Thank you.'

'What for?'

'Everything.' She stopped, as he turned to look at her.

'It's me who should be thanking you, I don't know what I'd have done if you hadn't stepped in to help out at the centre.'

'We were obviously meant to find each other then.'

'Lexie, you're amazing. I just wish—'

'Don't wish for anything else, let's just enjoy this while it lasts.' It was easier just to kiss him than face the truth. She was still hiding things from him, still saying the things that she wanted to believe were true; that she would still be able to walk away from Port Kara without her heart suffering another scar.

'The storm's broken.' Elliott finally pulled away from her, as another flash of lightning lit up the sky, a low rumble of thunder following in its wake. Within seconds rain was bouncing off the pavement, and Elliott put his arm around her shoulder. 'Come on, if we run, I can get you to the restaurant, before you get soaked to the skin.'

He did his best to protect her as they ran towards the pub on the other side of the harbour. Elliott had told her that The Crab and Winkle pub was owned by the same family that ran the two biggest crabbing boats out of Finbar Bay, and having lunch there would give them a good idea whether the reputation it had for sourcing the best crab in Cornwall was true.

'Are you okay?' Elliott pulled her into the pub doorway and Albie shook himself, showering them both with second-hand rain water.

'There was a bit of me that wasn't wet, but Albie's just taken care of that.' She laughed. 'I probably look like a drowned rat too.'

'You look great. But are you sure you want to go and eat like this? I don't want you to feel uncomfortable, sitting there in wet clothes.'

'I'm sure. I'll soon dry off. As long as you're sure they won't mind having Albie in the pub like that. I'm hoping he's already shaken off most of the water that's soaked into his coat.'

'I know James, the guy who runs the pub, and he said one half of the place is dog friendly. So as long as we stick to the right half, we should be fine.' Elliott smiled. 'And I've still got a pocket full of organic dog treats to keep him quiet. Because I know Albie's body is a temple.'

'More like a dustbin!' It was something else she liked about Elliott – how much he seemed to love Albie and vice versa. Dogs were supposed to be a good judge of character and, if that was true, then Elliott was definitely one of the good guys.

* * *

'So what do you think of the crab then?' Elliott put his knife and fork together and pushed his plate away.

'It's amazing. Everything tastes so fresh; I think it would be a great addition to the menu if we can get them to supply the centre.' Lexie's dress had finally dried out, but the rain was still battering against the window outside. The view across the harbour would probably have been beautiful if the weather had held out but, as it was, she could barely make out the lamp post on the pavement opposite.

'I was hoping we could take Albie for a walk on the beach this afternoon, but by the look of the weather, we'll be safer holed up here.'

'I'm in no hurry to go anywhere, and neither is Albie by the sounds of him.' Lexie laughed as the dog let out another loud snore. James had taken him up to the rooms above the pub, when they'd first arrived, to give him some lunch of his own and let him dry off. Back downstairs and with a full belly, in the warmth of the pub's family bar, he'd soon curled up for a sleep.

'Why are you in such a hurry to go back to London, then?' Elliott's question had come out of nowhere and she wasn't sure she could come up with an answer. Not one that would make sense to anyone else.

'It's just home.'

'It was.'

'I could ask you why you were so keen to leave.'

'You know the answer to that.'

'What would I do even if I stayed here?'

'I suppose it's too much to hope that you'd want to stay at the adventure centre?' Elliott reached out and touched her hand. 'You'd want more than that, wouldn't you?'

'I think the centre's brilliant, but I'm used to having my own business, and I can't imagine working for someone else long term.' It was a half-truth. The reality was that she couldn't really imagine working alongside anyone other than Finn, not long term. It would feel like another blight on his memory.

'I couldn't go back to working for someone else either, but that doesn't mean you've got to go it alone.' Elliott looked like he'd been about to say something else, when James pulled out a chair opposite Lexie and sat down.

'So, do you want Finbar Bay Fisheries to supply crab to the adventure centre?' He had a strong Cornish accent and he was straight down to business.

'I think we do, don't we?' Elliott looked across at Lexie.

'Yes, it'll make another fabulous addition to the menu.'

'Your other half knows what she's talking about.' James slapped his hand on the table. 'And you won't get better than the crab my brothers bring in. People come from miles around to eat here and it's all down to that.'

'We want to shift to a more local menu. Cornwall has got so much to offer.' Elliott didn't miss a beat this time, and he clearly wasn't going to bother to put James right about them not being married. He was obviously okay with it, and he seemed to understand why she didn't want to tell everyone about Finn.

'Who supplies the pork to the centre?' James looked at Lexie as he spoke.

'We've got a few suppliers including our local butcher in Port Kara, but I think breakfast is one of the areas where we could change a few things up to make a real impact. At the moment it's good, but what we really want is for it to be outstanding.' Lexie bit her lip. She'd caught herself saying '*we*' more and more often when she talked about the centre. But it wasn't her business and it wouldn't do her any favours to get more attached than she already had.

'There's a farmer out at Falstow who produces pork from rare breed free range pigs on 200 acres of woodland. You'll never have tasted bacon or sausages like it.' James grinned. 'It'll revolutionise your breakfasts.'

'That sounds amazing. Do you think we could squeeze in one more supplier visit tomorrow?' Lexie looked at Elliott. Spending time with him hadn't just reignited her passion for sourcing the very best ingredients possible, she was really enjoying all of it. Even getting soaked to the skin had been fun with Elliott.

'I wish we had the time to make it a whole week.' He sounded like he meant it, but she had a feeling that shopping around for suppliers for the centre would bore him long before it bored her. The lure of adventure would always be there for Elliott, just like it had been for Finn.

'I wish I'd had this sort of support from my wife when we were together.' James' Cornish accent made the statement sound sing-song, even as he frowned. 'She hated it when I was fishing and moaned like billy-o about all the time I spent on the boats with my brothers. Then I set this place up and she moaned that I was always in the bar, talking to customers. I couldn't do right for doing wrong, but the truth was she didn't get it. She didn't understand why the crabbing was so important to us and why I wanted to be part of that, either on the boats or selling the end product in the pub. She ran off with a double glazing salesman in the end, and I think she got the quiet life she always wanted. Not to mention the Victorian style conservatory she'd been harping on about for years!'

'Sorry.' Lexie had to fight the urge to laugh at the image of his ex-wife giving up his Cornish dreams for the conservatory of hers, but James and Elliott were smiling too.

'It's all right, she got her conservatory and I got the pub. We both got the lives we wanted in the end. I can't abide even looking at the bloody things now, though. My brother suggested we put on a conservatory out the back of the pub, for extra dining space and to give the customers a great view of the bay, but I'm not ready for that yet.' James grinned again. 'Still, you two seem to have it all. Let me go and get the number for the pig farm and you can give Barney a call, then we can talk terms on the crab.'

James got up and headed off through a door on the other side of the bar.

'Who'd have thought a conservatory could end a marriage?' Elliott smiled, his dark brown eyes filling with warmth.

'I've really enjoyed today.' Lexie let her fingers graze his, as she reached out for her glass.

'It's not over yet, we've still got tonight. And tomorrow.' Lexie nodded, unable to answer him as a lump formed in her throat. Tomorrow wasn't promised, she knew that as well as anyone. And, even if it came, it suddenly sounded far too short. Time didn't stop for anyone, and it wouldn't stop for her and Elliott, no matter how much she might want it to.

'I didn't think the rain was ever going to stop.' Lexie linked her arm through Elliott's as they walked down the path that ran alongside the river on the edge of Finbar Bay. The river fed into the estuary that led straight out to sea and was flanked on both sides by lush greenery, which looked almost tropical after the heavy rainfall. The trees were actually steaming now that the sun was out and Albie was wetter than ever from investigating the undergrowth, to see whether an unsuspecting rabbit might be hiding out in there from the aftermath of the storm.

'This is something else I love about living here. Most of the time the weather is brilliant and I can spend as much time outdoors as I like, but when the weather turns, it tends to be pretty dramatic.'

Elliott shrugged, knowing that Lexie understood, even if she kept insisting that London was where her heart was. She'd been so enthralled by everywhere they'd visited, and so fired up by the idea of running somewhere like the farm shop at Polton Dairy Farm, that he was sure she understood the pull of Cornwall. If anywhere could weave its magic and make her change her mind about leaving, it would be Cornwall itself. It wouldn't be Elliott; he couldn't offer her anything she really needed.

Even if he'd wanted to, he couldn't promise her what she had to hear to have any chance of convincing her to stay. He couldn't promise to take the safe path, or give up the life he loved, which was what he'd need to do to stop Lexie worrying every time he walked out the door. He'd spent years trying to live up to someone else's expectations and he'd been miserable the whole time. Even if Lexie wanted him to make those promises to her, he knew he couldn't keep them. It would be a strange kind of torture having her stay, but not be with him. Eventually whatever it was they had together would have to come to an end and, if she stayed in Port Kara, the chances were she'd find her Mr Steady, and Elliott would have to stand by and watch. But even that seemed preferable to her leaving altogether in less than a month. He'd miss her friendship most of all, so he was determined to make the most of it whilst it lasted.

'Albie seems to be having the time of his life.'

'He is, bless him.' Lexie grinned. 'The poor thing's got no clue that, even if he does manage to flush out a rabbit, he'll never catch it whilst he's on this wander lead.'

No sooner had she spoken, than something rustled in the bushes just up ahead of them. A black ball of fur shot out of the undergrowth and Albie surged forward as far as his wander lead would let him go, pulling Lexie and Elliott forward in the process.

As Albie almost reached the black blur that was now his prey, it shot to the left, landing in the river with a loud splash. Throwing Albie's lead at Elliott, before he even had a chance to react, Lexie ran forward, and seconds later there was an even louder splash. She was in the water too.

'What the hell are you doing? Are you okay?' Elliott ran to the end of the river bank, still keeping a firm hold of Albie, who looked like he might join Lexie in the water at any moment. The water was running fast, but Lexie had already managed to get to the edge, with the ball of black fluff under her arm.

'It disappeared under the water and I didn't want it to drown. I think it's a dog.' Lexie's hair was plastered to the side of her head and she was covered in green algae.

'It could have been a badger for all you knew.' Elliott quickly tied Albie's lead to a tree on the edge of the bank, and reached out his arms towards Lexie.

'It doesn't matter, I still didn't want it to drown.'

'It would probably have sunk its teeth into you if it had been, rather than shown you any thanks for saving it.' He didn't want to admit that he'd probably have jumped in, if Lexie hadn't been so quick, even it had just been a rabbit. His heart had been in his mouth for the couple of seconds when he hadn't been able to see her in the fast flowing river. 'You could have drowned.'

'I'm fine. I think adrenaline just took over.' She fell against him as he pulled her and the little dog clear of the water. 'I don't think this little chap would have lasted long. He feels like a bag of bones.'

'Let's take a look at him.' Elliott lifted the dog out of her arms. She was right, there was nothing to him, and there were bald patches obvious even in the wet coat that clung to his tiny body. 'He looks like a stray to me and he's not wearing a collar.'

'What are we going to do with him? We can't just leave him here. He might be hurt too.'

'If you're sure you're okay, we can go back into Finbar Bay and ask James whether there's a vet who can check if he's microchipped.' Elliott turned the little dog over in his arms. 'He's a she, by the way!'

'Oh poor little girl.' Lexie nodded her head. 'I'm fine, I just want to get her checked over.'

'We can ask James to ring the local council too and see if anyone has reported their dog missing and then share her picture on the centre's social media pages, once she's dry and a bit more recognisable to whoever might have lost her.'

'And what if no one comes forward to claim her?' Lexie looked like she might burst into tears at the thought.

'We'll cross that bridge when we come to it.' Holding the shivering dog closer to him to try and warm her up, Elliott could feel her little heart thudding under his hand. She didn't look well cared for and, if he'd been a betting man, he'd have gambled a big stake that no one would come forward to claim her. But, if they didn't, he'd already made up his mind he was going to keep her. She'd landed in their lives unexpectedly, in much the same way that Lexie had landed in his. He had no choice but to let Lexie go when she was ready, but he could keep the little dog they'd found together. Animals didn't bring the same complications into your life that people did. He only had to look at how much Albie meant to Lexie. He'd seen a new side to her, though. She'd been fearless when it came to jumping into the river to save the dog. That made her ten times braver than his clients, who took part in engineered adrenaline highs, that were carefully monitored and controlled by well qualified guides. There was a tiny bit of him that couldn't help holding on to the hope that maybe she'd learn to embrace adventure too, and make a life in Port Kara after all. Except hope could end up being far more dangerous than any adrenaline high, if you let it.

9

The population of Port Kara seemed to increase on an almost daily basis as the school holidays got into full swing. Having Myrtle Cottage to hide out in was more of a haven than ever for Lexie, but there were times when she wanted to wander among the crowds in the quaint little high street that looked like something taken straight from a postcard. She'd got into the habit of eating at the adventure centre most days but there were still times when she needed to stock up on supplies for the cottage, so she'd had a list of things to get in the village when she had a rare morning off.

'You're looking more like a local every time I see you!' Morwenna called out, as she emerged from the newsagents clutching a copy of the local newspaper and a family-sized bar of chocolate. She was wearing one of her trademark headscarves, this time covered in pictures of beach huts, and the ready smile that rarely seemed to leave her face.

'I almost feel like one too.' Lexie laughed as she drew level with her. 'Especially when I get a surge of impatience at all these visitors clogging up the pavements in the high street! Which is a bit of a cheek when you consider that I'm just a visitor too.'

'I don't think you are, not any more. The Cornish summer's kiss has given you more of a glow than any holiday-maker could ever achieve, despite you being shut up in that kitchen for so many hours every day.'

'It's all the long walks on the beach with Albie.'

'And the rest.' Morwenna dropped one of her perfect winks, and Lexie suspected she was the one person who'd seen through the pretence that she and Elliott were still just colleagues. She'd never come out and said it, though, which Lexie was grateful for.

'Are you not opening the shop today then?'

'I will later.' Morwenna patted the bar of chocolate she was holding. 'I've got a few jobs to do and then I was going to sit somewhere quiet with the paper and work my way through a few rows of creamy milk chocolate. It's the breakfast of kings!'

'Sounds good to me.' Lexie laughed again. 'Don't you ever think about getting a bit of help in the shop, though, so you can keep it open more often and have more time to yourself?'

'People find me when they need me.' Morwenna tapped the side of her nose. 'Now, can I interest you in accompanying me on a quick tour of Port Kara's premier retailers? I've got to get to the butchers and the bakers, although sadly we've not got a candlestick makers to complete the set these days.'

'I need to nip into the butchers too.' Lexie pulled a face. 'Although to be honest, I'm more interested in having a chat with Jory, to see if I can work out why he still hasn't asked Vyvyan out. She's all but given up on him, I think, but he's got no idea what he's missing out on.'

'Indeed he hasn't and it's a mystery to me too.' Morwenna turned in the direction of the butchers, gesturing with her head for Lexie to follow her. 'Perhaps it's time we gave the two of them a helping hand.'

'I thought you didn't believe in pushing people? You've said to me more than once that only I'll know what decisions are right for me.'

'That's true, most of the time. But every so often, when words of advice aren't enough, I've been known to give the people who come to me for help a gentle shove in the right direction.'

'But you said she just needed to be authentic and he'd see who she was and ask her out.'

'If Vyvyan insists on putting on an act, then surely it's up to those of us who really know her to set him straight?'

Lexie wasn't going to argue with her. It might not be the message that Morwenna had been giving her from the first day they'd met, but they both wanted Vyvyan to be happy. If Jory was too shy to ask her out, and with Vyvyan steadfastly refusing to make the first move, then they could be at an impasse forever. So Morwenna could be forgiven for pushing her principles to one side, just this once.

'Morning Jory!' Morwenna strode straight towards the counter. Having made up her mind to finally give them a push, she clearly wasn't going to waste any time.

'Morning Mor.' Jory nodded in greeting, and Lexie tried to concentrate on not breathing through her nose. For a chef, she'd never been keen on the smell of raw meat and standing in a butcher's shop for any length of time made her feel a bit queasy. Vyvyan must really like Jory to spend as much time hanging around in his shop as she did. 'What can I get you this morning?'

'I'd like some belly of pork please, enough for two, and a pound of those chipolata sausages, the ones you make on site.'

'Right-o, anything else? What about some of this lovely rib eye steak, it's on special this week?'

'No, just the sausages and pork belly, thanks.' Morwenna paused, and Lexie wondered for a moment whether she'd thought better of her plan to give Jory a push. 'Oh there is one more thing...'

'What's that, my love?' Jory had his back to her, weighing out the sausages on the scale.

'I was just wondering why you've never got around to asking my cousin, Vyvyan, out?' Morwenna didn't drop her gaze, even as he turned towards her, his mouth hanging open in surprise. 'You must know she likes you? She's in here often enough and no one buys that many pork chops.'

'Well I did think that, and for a while there I hoped it was because she liked me, but I've never wanted to ask her out whilst she was in the shop. It would be embarrassing for me if she said no, in front of the other customers or the lads that work here, and I didn't want her to feel forced into saying yes because she was too nice to say no to my face.'

'Ever heard of such a thing as a telephone?'

Vyvyan's patience with Jory might finally be running out after five years, but Lexie had no idea how Morwenna had managed to stop herself intervening for as long as she had, listening to her now.

'Of course I have, and I tried it a few times over the years. I never spoke to Vyvyan, mind, it was always her sister, Pat. She'd either say she'd pass the message on and I never heard back, or other times she'd tell me that Vyvyan was seeing someone else, or it was still too soon after her losing her husband.'

'I see.' Morwenna looked over at Lexie, an unspoken understanding passing between them. 'I'm sorry to have put you on the spot like that, Jory, but I think Vyvyan would be more than happy to go out with you, if you were to ask her face to face.'

'But her sister, Pat—'

'You leave Pat to me; I'll get to the bottom of the miscommunication between them. You just concentrate on Vyvyan.' Morwenna handed him a ten pound note, in exchange for her purchases, and he passed over the change.

'Are you sure she'll really want to?' Jory still didn't seem convinced, but Morwenna nodded.

'Just get it done, Jory, and you'll wish you'd asked her face to face years ago, I promise.'

'All right then, I will.' He turned to Lexie, who was still trying to process it all. 'Now what can I get you, my love, or are you just here to give me some relationship advice too?'

'I'll have a pound of those sausages as well, please, and a couple of pieces of that rib eye steak.' It wasn't what Lexie had planned to come in for, but she just wanted to go back outside with Morwenna, so they could talk about what had happened. Less than two minutes later, she was outside the shop and relieved to see Morwenna still waiting for her on the pavement.

'What did you make of that, then?' The older woman knitted her eyebrows together as she looked at Lexie. 'It seems there's been a third party putting a spanner in the works all along.'

'I can't understand it, Pat knows how long Vyvyan has been interested in Jory. They always seem so close, despite the teasing. I can't imagine why Pat would have done that.'

'It's because of that closeness, though, sweetheart. Pat must be terrified, if Vyvyan and Jory get together, that she might become surplus to requirements.'

'But even when Vyvyan was married, they were all still together.' Lexie felt sorry for both sisters, but in very different ways, and she could understand the feeling of not wanting to be left alone all too well.

'True, but Phil understood their relationship. He'd been friends with both of them from right back to their primary school days. A lot of men wouldn't have wanted Pat hanging around, though, and I'm guessing she's terrified that Jory might feel that way.'

'What are you going to do? If he asks Vyvyan out face to face, and she says yes, he's bound to tell her eventually about the phone calls asking her out over the years.'

'I don't know yet, but I'll figure it out.' She squeezed Lexie's arm. 'Can I count on your help if I need it?'

'Of course you can.'

'Thank you, sweetheart.' She gave Lexie's arm another squeeze. 'None of us want you to leave Port Kara, you know that don't you?'

'I do.' Lexie didn't know what else to say, especially as the idea of leaving a place that was increasingly starting to feel like home terrified her too. But Morwenna wasn't going to intervene and force her to stay, like she'd all but forced Jory to ask Vyvyan out. As long as the decision was all up to Lexie, she didn't think she'd ever be able to make it. She was still hoping for some sort of sign, though, something to convince her once and for all that staying in Cornwall was the right thing to do.

* * *

Albie raced across the sand and Lexie held her breath, hoping that her new found trust in him wouldn't be misplaced and that he'd come back when she called. Leaping onto the tennis ball he was chasing, he skidded to a halt, sending up a shower of sand.

'Come on Albie, come on Splash, back you come.' Albie turned and looked at her, before galloping back in her direction, the little black dog she'd rescued from the river in Finbar Bay following hot on his heels.

'My dog seems to be a good influence on yours.' Elliott laughed. 'He actually seems to prefer chasing around with her now, rather than mugging holiday makers for their picnics.'

'I know, but I still think he might let me down every time I risk it. Especially after he leapt into the sea after you that day.'

'He's not the only one capable of leaping into the water unexpectedly.' Elliott caught hold of her hand and pulled her towards him, so that they were standing face to face. 'But I'm glad you did. I couldn't imagine life without Splash now.'

'I guess I'm just lucky that didn't end up being my nickname, seeing as I made a much bigger splash than she did when I hit the water.' She shivered, as he pushed a strand of hair behind her ear.

'That's not the first thing that springs to mind when I think about you.'

'I'm glad you decided to adopt Splash when no one came forward to claim her; she deserved a second chance and I can't think of anyone better to give it to her than you.'

'Like you told me once before, everyone deserves a second chance.' He had an intense look in his eyes and the tick-tock of the time slipping away, until her lease of the cottage was over, was getting almost deafening. She'd been struggling to know how to respond, when the sound of a seagull squawking overhead made her pull away and look up; the real world always found a way of crashing in.

'Have you got time to come to mine for a drink?' Lexie clipped on Albie's lead when they were about a hundred yards away from the cottage, she didn't want to risk the dog running off at the last minute, which he might well do if he realised their walk with Splash and Elliott was nearly over.

'I can always make time.' Elliott was due back at the centre for the welcome dinner with a new group of guests and she was gradually trying to pull back from running the restaurant, doing less shifts, and leaving Billy to supervise the agency staff on his own for more of the time.

Elliott followed her up the path to the cottage, and she handed him Albie's lead as she unlocked the front door. It had almost become a routine since he'd decided to keep Splash, the two of them meeting to walk the dogs on the beach every day, once the tourists had started to pack up and empty the car park, leaving the mile and a half long stretch of sand, that was Port Kara's main beach, almost deserted. She loved that time of day better than any other and it was something else she'd miss when she got back to London. Considering that Albie had nearly been responsible for Splash drowning, the two dogs were now best of friends, and he'd definitely miss her too. It was funny how quickly somewhere could come to feel like home, and Myrtle Cottage was the closest thing they'd had to that since selling the business. She and Finn had lived in the flat above the restaurant, with Albie, but when she'd sold up she'd taken out a rental lease on a furnished flat, putting most of their stuff into storage until she decided where to put down proper roots. There was a two-bedroomed terraced cottage she'd seen in Blackheath, with an astronomical rent and a little garden that might cheer Albie up a bit when he was missing the beach. She'd seen it online, and it had reminded her of Myrtle Cottage just enough for her to email the agent and offer a rental deposit without even seeing the place. It wouldn't be the same, but they'd moved on before and survived, so they could do it again. She'd already given notice on the other flat, so they should be moved in by October, and someone else would be enjoying the view from Myrtle Cottage out over Port Kara beach by then.

'I bet you never thought this would be your life, did you?' Lexie laughed, as she brought the coffees back into the living room. Splash was laid out across Elliott's legs, and Albie was lying on his feet. He couldn't have moved if he'd wanted to and she wondered if the dogs had picked up on something, wanting to keep him there as much as she did. But his duty to the centre would be calling soon and he'd leave, no matter how hard Albie and Splash tried to stop him. It was like a siren's call to the sailors of old.

'I have to say I didn't. I've never even thought about getting a dog before, but I'd already fallen for Albie, so when Splash turned up it seemed like it was meant to be.' Elliott shrugged. 'I'd never have had a dog when I was working such long hours in London, it wouldn't have been fair, and I never had any pets as a kid because Dad hates them.'

'How can anyone hate dogs?' Lexie set the cups down on the coffee table and sat next to Elliott on the sofa.

'He hates anything that doesn't have a purpose in his eyes, and for him that's anything that costs money rather than makes it.'

'What about your mum?'

'She's got three cats now. And a tattoo.' Elliott laughed. 'Dad hated cats even more than dogs, and he told her if she ever got a tattoo he'd divorce her. So the first thing she did, when they finally split up, was to go out and get a tattoo, and within three weeks she'd bought three kittens from the same litter, too.'

'Does she regret it now?'

'Getting the kittens or the tattoo?'

'No.' Lexie laughed and shook her head, wondering if the question she was about to ask was too personal. 'I meant does she regret staying in the marriage for so long?'

'I should think so and I wish she hadn't. I wish I'd stood up to him when I was younger too and had the guts to tell him I didn't want to be a carbon copy of him.'

'But then you wouldn't have ended up here, or been the person you are.'

'Maybe.'

'I'm glad you're here and that you turned out the way you did.' As Lexie reached out for his hand, Splash jumped off his lap.

'I'm glad you're here too.' He took her hand in his as he spoke and she tried not to think about the reason she was in Port Kara, and what Finn would say if he knew how close she and Elliott had become. But then she realised she couldn't imagine it even if she'd wanted to, because she couldn't remember what her husband's voice had sounded like any more. There was no hiding from it any more. Elliott was gradually pushing him out, and she had to do something about it before it was too late.

The hammering on the door of Elliott's flat was so frantic, he'd half expected to be able to smell smoke when he opened it. Instead it was Lexie standing there, her face as white as the surf that turned over with the incoming tide on Port Kara beach.

'Are you okay? You look terrible.' Elliott stood back as she charged into the flat, Albie right behind her and a black laptop bag clutched to her chest.

'I feel terrible. I've lost everything and I can't even remember what he sounds like.' Lexie took a shuddering breath, her voice breaking on the words.

'Do you mean Finn?' Elliott knew the answer before she even nodded. But she wasn't making any sense and he needed her to slow down if he was going to try and help her.

'I realised tonight, after you left, that I was forgetting things about him. I tried to imagine talking to him again, like I used to when he first died, but I couldn't even remember what his voice sounded like.' Her face was wet with tears now and the words were still coming out in a rush.

'You're probably just panicking and it's making you think that you can't.' It was hard to know what to say without making things worse. He knew how badly losing Finn had affected her, but he'd never seen her grief this naked before and it twisted something deep inside. How could he help her, when all she really wanted was Finn?

'I'm not imagining it; I really can't remember what he sounded like. I wanted to watch one of the videos I had of him on the laptop, just so I could hear him again. But the files have corrupted and it's all gone.' The last word turned into a sob and Albie was pacing up and down, not knowing how to comfort Lexie any more than Elliott did. At least he could try something practical.

'Can I take a look?'

'You can, but there's an error message coming up that looks like a no entry sign, every time I try to open one of the files.'

'Let me get you a drink and you can sit down and try to relax, while I see if I can work out what's wrong.'

'I don't want a drink.' Lexie was shaking her head. 'Please just have a look at it and see if there's anything you can do.'

'There must be other copies of some of the videos, did you upload any of them to social media sites?'

'A few and there'll be some that other people might have kept a copy of. But I'm the only one with copies of all of them. When I changed my phone, after Finn died, I just uploaded the video files from the phone onto my laptop. It was so stupid; I should have made copies straight away.'

'Don't worry, it'll be okay,' Elliott just hoped that wasn't a lie. He'd rather have a cliff face to scale down any day; this had far higher stakes.

'Any luck yet?' Lexie barely gave him sixty seconds before she started asking the question, leaning over his shoulder and fidgeting from foot to foot.

'Just give me a minute.' He held his breath as he waited for the computer to load a webpage, and the log in name automatically loaded. 'Do you know the password you used for the storage cloud?'

'I think it's Albie123, with a capital A.' Lexie was still looking over his shoulder, as he entered the details.

'Is this one of the videos?' He clicked on a MP4 video file and an image of Finn running towards the sea, with a surfboard under his arm and Albie at his feet, filled the screen. Elliott watched the video with a weird mixture of relief at having located a back-up copy of the files, and a twinge of irrational jealousy. It was crazy to be jealous of Albie chasing after Finn, but it was another reminder that Lexie had shared a life with someone else. A man she'd still be devoted to, if he'd lived. He hated himself for it, especially when Lexie was so happy he'd managed to recover the files.

'Thank you.' She leant over the back of the chair, and kissed his cheek. It was just a brief brush of the lips and she took the laptop off him in a single move. The sound of Finn's laughter filled the space between them and, when he turned to look at her, she was staring at the screen as if there was nothing else in the world.

'Do you want that drink now?'

'Uh-huh.' She didn't look up at him, as she sank into one of the other armchairs, loading another video of Finn.

'What can I get you? A coffee, or a glass of wine?'

'Whatever you're having, I don't care.' She meant the drink, he knew she did, but he couldn't help thinking that the statement was loaded with so much more. All she'd wanted was to hear Finn's voice again and he realised, like a punch to the gut, that she'd never care that much about him. He was just a way to spend the summer, someone to pass the time with. She'd already met the love of her life and he'd been too late. As much as he wanted to tell himself that it didn't matter, and that he'd always known they'd end when the summer did, there was a hollow feeling in his chest that hadn't been there before.

10

'Are you sure this is a good idea?' Lexie stirred the pot of crab soup that was slowly warming on the oven top. 'Vyvyan's still not speaking to Pat, is she?'

'That's why this is perfect.' Morwenna was arranging stems of jasmine in a large glass vase. 'Pat doing all of this and making sure that Vyvyan and Jory have the perfect date, is the ideal way of apologising, and Vyvyan will have no choice but to forgive her.'

'And what about Jory?' Lexie had heard all about the fall-out when Vyvyan had finally discovered her sister's deception. Morwenna had confronted Pat about it, and she'd been spot on about why Pat had been so determined to keep Vyvyan and Jory apart. When Vyvyan had announced that Jory had finally asked her out, on her latest trip to stock up on pork chops, Pat had decided that honesty was the best policy. Vyvyan hadn't taken it as well as they'd hoped, though, and the sisters hadn't spoken for the best part of a week. Now everyone's hopes for a reconciliation were pinned on pulling off the perfect first date for Vyvyan and Jory.

'He's fully on board.' Morwenna stood back to admire the floral display she'd created for the centre of the table. 'When I explained to him why Pat didn't pass on his messages, he was sympathetic. He's been on his own since his mother died. He never got married like his older brothers and he's been lonely in the years since she died, so he could understand why Pat did what she did.'

'I just hope Vyvyan comes around to that way of thinking.' Lexie was confident of pulling off the menu, but the rest was out of her hands. After the soup, they'd be serving fillet of beef, with buttered Cornish new potatoes and spinach, and they'd finish with dark chocolate brownies served with home-made pistachio ice cream. Pat and Elliott were waiting the table and serving drinks, and Morwenna had been put in charge of the floral display and table decorations. 'How's Jory persuading her to come up to the adventure centre, if she's still not speaking to Pat?'

'He's told her that Elliott is having a reception for local retailers and promised her that Pat won't be here.' Morwenna grinned. 'So by the end of the evening, they'll either all be friends again, or Vyvyan won't be speaking to any of us, even Jory!'

'I've just seen Jory's car pull into the car park.' Elliott stuck his head around the door of the kitchen. 'So we'll be action stations in about five minutes!'

'I'd better bring the flowers out then.' Morwenna picked up the vase, the smell of jasmine competing with the aroma of the food as she did. 'Let's just hope Pat's not wearing the contents of this vase in the next five minutes.'

'How's it going out there so far?' Lexie added a swirl of fresh cream, basil leaves and black pepper to the soup as Elliott waited to take the starters out to their VIP guests.

'Well Vyvyan's either putting on a show for Jory's sake, or her feelings towards Pat are softening.' He looked as relieved as she felt.

He was obviously fond of the sisters and they were more than just staff to him. 'Morwenna has headed off to let them get on with it. This might have been her and Pat's idea, but I don't think she could bear to stand around and watch it all unfold.'

'Scaredy cat!' Lexie returned his smile, briefly wondering what Elliott's father might make of his willingness to act the part of waiter, in an attempt to sort out the problems of the hired help, as he'd no doubt see it. She wasn't sure Finn would have been willing to do the same, unless there was a celebrity client thrown into the equation.

'If we can get through the soup without it ending up in anyone's lap, then I think we're onto a winner.' Elliott lifted up the bowls. 'If I'm not back in twenty minutes for the main course, you might need to come out and referee. Either that or book them a slot on the Jeremy Kyle show so they can slug it out, live on daytime TV.'

'I'll keep an eye on the clock and I'll google Jeremy Kyle's number while I'm waiting.'

As it turned out, there was no need to referee and when Lexie snuck a look out into the dining room in between the main course and dessert, everything looked to be going to plan. Vyvyan was laughing at something Jory had said but, even better, was the sight of her giving her sister a quick thumbs up.

'Thanks so much for this.' Pat, who was usually by far the least demonstrative of the sisters, put an arm around Lexie's waist, when she came out into the kitchen, just after dessert was served.

'Anytime, I'm just glad it worked out okay.'

'Me too. I think I'm fully forgiven, which is more than I deserve, and a lot of that is down to how fantastic your menu is. It's got all of Vyvyan's favourites in it and using the meat from Jory's shop for the main course was a stroke of genius.'

'Are you okay, though?' Lexie looked at Pat, who nodded in response.

'I'm feeling better than I have in years. In fact, I'm just off on a date of my own.'

'Are you? Who with?' Lexie tried and failed not to sound so surprised.

'I'm going over to Jasper Holland's place for a late supper.' Pat's tone was nonchalant, as if that was the sort of thing she did every day. But if Lexie hadn't been wedged between her and the kitchen counter, she might have fallen over.

'*The* Jasper Holland?'

'Yes, I know he's got a reputation for dating a string of bimbos, but we got talking when me and Vyvyan went over there, after Elliott rescued that young chap from the sea. Turns out we like a lot of the same books and classic movies, and maybe he just wanted to talk to someone closer to his own age for once. I must make him feel quite young!'

'Wow, you're certainly a dark horse, Pat.'

'I expect I'm just a bit different to what he's used to and he'll be back to the bimbos next week, but either way I'm glad it all came out with Vyvyan and Jory.' Pat fixed her with a serious look. 'Sometimes you have to let people go, to be able to move on with your own life. If Vyvyan and Jory decide they want to be together, and there's no room for me, then I'll just have to learn to live with it. Hanging onto Vyvyan for dear life was killing us both. I was eaten up with guilt about keeping Jory's interest in her a secret for almost five years, and she was miserable, yearning for something she thought she'd never have. Sometimes you just have to let yourself move on, Lexie, and try something new.'

'Have you been taking lessons from Morwenna?'

'No, just from life.' Pat gave her waist another squeeze. 'Just make sure you aren't as blind as I was, and that you let go of the past before you risk your future.'

'It's not always easy, is it?'

'Nothing worth doing is ever easy. I'll see you later, my love.' Pat planted a kiss on her cheek and Lexie carried on with cleaning the kitchen. Maybe it was finally time to make a clean start with her life too, if she could just let go of the past for long enough.

* * *

Billy's singing wasn't nearly as good as his cooking skills, but that didn't stop him belting out every song that came onto the radio, and Lexie couldn't stop herself laughing as he tried to hit the high note in a Sia song that the local DJ had described as her biggest hit.

'Have you ever had singing lessons?' She looked over at him, as she took a punnet of raspberries out of the fridge, and he shook his head. 'Well maybe you should think about it!'

'Cheeky!' Billy grinned and responded by belting out the final chorus with even more enthusiasm.

'Thank goodness for that. A bit of respite at last.' Lexie let out a low whistle, as the DJ announced that the news was up next.

'The headlines at four on Three Ports Radio.' The newsreader had a more serious tone than the DJ, but the big local news was never anything very troubling. 'The international surfing festival at Port Tremellien has been hit by a tragedy with the death of an unnamed surfer.'

'Oh God.' Lexie dropped the punnet of raspberries, sending them scattering across the kitchen work station. Her neck prickled as the newsreader carried on, and Billy seemed to freeze on the spot.

'Eye witnesses say that the surfer was leading a group and was knocked unconscious when two of the competitors collided. Attempts to resuscitate the man, who is said to be a local resident in his mid-thirties, were unsuccessful, and paramedics pronounced him dead at the scene. Police say the man won't be named until his next of kin have been informed.'

'It won't be Elliott, Lexie. There are hundreds of people at the festival, and Elliott's too good at what he does to be caught up in something like that.'

'Finn was good at what he did, too.' She couldn't stop shivering and, as she looked at Billy, he seemed to be going in and out of focus. She had a horrible feeling she might be about to pass out.

'I'll get you a chair, I think you need to sit down.' He ran out to the restaurant and came back with one of the dining chairs twenty seconds later.

'I'm okay.'

'No, you're not. Sit down before you fall down.' Billy more or less forced her into the chair, even as she continued shaking her head.

'This can't be happening again.'

'It isn't. I know Elliott and the rest of the team who've gone down to Port Tremellien today. They're all professionals, they do this stuff for a living, they know the risks and they know how to avoid them.'

'But what if it is him? Can you try ringing?'

Poor Billy, he looked almost as bad as she felt. He probably had no idea what to do with a hysterical woman, so he must have been relieved to have the excuse to go off and make the call. 'I'll go and use the phone in the restaurant and see whether any of the bar staff have heard something from one of the guides.'

'Okay.' Lexie couldn't stay sitting down. The waiting was worse than anything, and the DJ had put a feel-good summer song on straight after the news report. Yanking the lead out of the radio, she started to put the raspberries back into the punnet. Half of them were already too damaged to be used, crushed by their fall onto the hard surface, just like Finn had been. Was Elliott lying somewhere now, cold and lifeless? She couldn't go through it again.

'I left a message for him, but there haven't been any calls into the centre. I'm sure if something bad had happened we'd have heard by now.' Billy's words were obviously intended to be reassuring, as he came back into the kitchen, but the look on his face told another story. He was worried too.

'I hope you're right, but I can't think straight. Can you manage the rest of the prep, if I go up to the flat and check on the dogs? I think I'll be more of a hindrance than a help to you otherwise.' Lexie turned to the young sous chef and he nodded.

'No problem, we've already done most of the prep anyway. If a call comes through to the bar to confirm that Elliott and the others are okay, I'll come up and find you.'

'Thanks.' Lexie touched his shoulder as she moved past him, hoping that he couldn't feel her shaking.

Opening the door of the flat, less than a minute later, Albie lifted his head off the sofa to acknowledge her presence and then stretched out again, making the most of the fact that Splash wasn't taking up the space beside him. The little black dog was pawing at the full-length windows, which looked out over the beach, and she started to whine as soon as she spotted Lexie.

'You know, don't you?' She bent down and scooped up the dog. Maybe she was reading too much into it, but weren't animals supposed to have a sixth sense about this sort of thing? Albie always seemed to pick up on it when she was upset, but this time he seemed more interested in making the most of the sunny spot by the window.

Sitting down on the sofa with Splash still in her arms, she checked her phone. She'd texted Elliott on the way up to the flat to tell him to ring her as soon as he got the message. She must have checked for a reply at least a hundred times over the next half an hour, and she felt like hurling her phone out of the window and over the cliff when there was still no response.

'Lexie.' Elliott was suddenly standing in the doorway of the flat, his expression more serious than normal.

'I thought you were dead!' Splash jumped off her lap, before she could even stand up, and hurtled towards Elliott like a bullet out of a gun.

'I'm sorry, I tried to call, but it was chaos at Port Tremellien with everything that happened, and then I couldn't get a signal.'

'Are you okay, is everyone else okay?' She walked towards him, her legs shaking, terrified that she might just have conjured him up and he wouldn't really be there.

'No one from the centre was involved in the accident, we weren't even in the water at the time it happened. The group we were leading were all in the amateur round, but it was a group of professionals trying to qualify for a place in the World Series who had the accident. We were just watching and thinking how amazing they were, and suddenly all hell broke loose.'

'Did you actually see the accident?'

'We tried to help out with first aid when they brought him onto the beach, but there was nothing anyone could do.'

'Oh God.'

'I'm sorry I scared you again.'

'I can't keep doing this Elliott.' Lexie turned away from him. If she looked at his face, she wouldn't be able to say what she had to say. 'I promised myself I wouldn't get involved with anyone who got their kicks from putting their life on the line again, but all you've done since I met you is take risks. Rescuing that guy from the sea at Jasper's beach party was bad enough, but then I have to hear on the radio that there's been another surfing accident when you're there. It wasn't you this time, but it easily could have been. And it might be next time.'

'I was never in any danger rescuing that guy from the beach. Like I said at the time, he was just an idiot who'd drunk too much and got himself into trouble because he didn't take advice. I'm always careful and follow all the safety procedures. Nothing bad is *ever* going to happen to me; it's not going to happen to you again, either.' Elliott echoed Billy's words, as he moved to stand behind her, and she had to fight the urge to turn and let him put his arms around her. It would have been so easy to let him comfort her. Nothing could happen to someone like him – except it could – and lying to herself wasn't going to work any more. She cared about him. A lot. But she couldn't lose someone she loved again. It was too late to stop herself from falling in love with him, as hard as she'd tried, but she could control when it ended if she walked away now.

'You can't make me that promise, no one can.'

'I could stop doing all the things I love and get hit by a car, or fall down and hit my head walking Splash, or get ill completely out of the blue. None of us can make the promise to always be there for someone else, Lexie, even if we want that more than anything else.' He took hold of her shoulders turning her to face him, even as she tried to resist. 'But we said we'd make the most of whatever time we have together and that's all anyone can really promise. It was only supposed to be the summer, but I don't think that's going to be enough for me. I want you to stay and I promise you I will be here for you as long as I can. Seeing what happened on the beach today made me realise something; I want to be with you.'

'I want to be with you, too.' Tears were streaming down her face and Splash was whining again. Even Albie had got up from his spot in the sun, to see what was going on.

'So we've got to make this work, right?' Elliott's voice was gentle and she found herself nodding, even though she knew it never could. The guilt of growing so close to him had almost crippled her, but it was hearing about the accident on the radio that had shattered her last bit of hope into a million pieces. She could never stay with Elliott, not if she wanted to survive. If she stayed, he'd feel suffocated, and she'd be terrified every time he went to work. Somehow she'd find the courage to tell him that she was going and make him understand that it was the best thing for both of them.

* * *

Lexie couldn't move. She was trying to run towards the sea, but her legs wouldn't co-operate. Elliott had broken his promise, it was happening again, he was in the water and she was the only one who could save him.

'No!' Lexie jolted awake as her body jerked in response to the nightmare. It had felt so real that it took her a moment or two to realise where she was. In bed, in Myrtle Cottage, and Elliott was safe. But for how long?

Getting into the shower she let the hot water run, not wanting to face the day. She had to leave, it was so clear now, and even though that had been her plan all along, it was gut wrenching. Leaving Elliott and everyone else in Port Kara, who she'd come to love, was going to be awful. But still not as bad as living every second when he was out, on some adrenaline adventure or another, waiting for that call. He was at far more risk than Finn had ever been, because he put other people before his own safety. Finn had only ever had himself to look out for, and it had still ended badly.

At least she'd be leaving the kitchen at the centre in good hands. Billy had really risen to the challenge and his college had agreed he could finish his qualifications by distance learning, so he'd be able to head up the catering team most of the time. They'd found a couple of agency staff who worked well, and she hoped at least one of them would be willing to take on a permanent position. The last thing she wanted to do was leave Elliott in the lurch.

She got dressed almost robotically; it was like she was closing off her feelings already. How many more mornings would she get up and look at the view across the beach from Myrtle Cottage to the headland where the centre was? Less than she could count on one hand if either of the agency staff agreed to step in. The adventure centre was Elliott's responsibility, but she wanted to be the one to make the call. Letting him know what she was doing would give him a chance to try and change her mind, and every time she looked at him her resolve weakened. She had to make it a fait accompli, it was the only way. Ten minutes later it was done. She'd offered the job of assistant head chef to one of the agency staff, who'd happily accepted, and had arranged for some additional cover from the agency to start the next day. There was no going back now. It was over, just as she'd known it always would be. Only back then she'd had no idea how much it would hurt.

Elliott had woken up on Sunday with that same uneasy feeling in his chest as he'd had when he'd witnessed Lexie's reaction to losing the videos of Finn. It was a sort of hollow feeling he couldn't explain, like something essential to his happiness had disappeared. But Lexie was still in the centre's kitchen when he walked in later that morning, just as he'd expected her to be, making the final breakfasts for the guests about to check out. He enjoyed watching her work, especially when she didn't know he was there. Tucking a strand of hair that had escaped from her pony tail, behind her ear, she took a tray of fresh Danish pastries out of the oven and set them down on the stainless steel surface, before turning and catching sight of him. He had to persuade her to stay, no matter what it cost.

'You shouldn't sneak up on a woman when she's carrying a burning hot tray.'

'It's a risk I'm willing to take.' He wanted to reach out to her, but Billy was only a few feet away, cooking up a storm of bacon and eggs. In the end they hadn't managed to keep their relationship outside work a complete secret from the other staff at the centre, but they'd played it down, and public displays of affection were definitely not on the agenda.

'What are you doing this afternoon?' Lexie put the pastries onto a cooling tray as she spoke.

'Hoping you might be free?' They'd got into the habit of spending every Sunday afternoon and evening together, as it was the only time they were completely free of commitments at the centre.

'I thought we could have a picnic on the cliffs above Dagger's Head? The forecast looks good and I want to make the most of the last days of summer, before we have to give in and admit that autumn is here.'

'Me too.' The hollow feeling in his chest intensified. It was already September and he knew her lease only ran for a little bit longer. But he still had time to change her mind and he was banking on it. She wasn't the only one who wanted to put the last days of summer to good use. 'I'll be in the office doing some paperwork, come and find me when you're ready.'

'Okay.' Lexie turned back to what she was doing and he tried to look forward to the afternoon he was spending with her, but he just couldn't shake the feeling of dread that seemed to have taken up permanent residence in his chest.

The pile of paperwork in his office was something he hated doing at the best of times, but it was doubly difficult when all his mind seemed determined to focus on was ways to persuade Lexie to stay. He was looking at a row of figures for the fourth time, trying to take them in, when his mobile rang.

'Hello, Dorton's Adventure Centre.'

'Is that Elliott Dorton?' It was a woman's voice, but he didn't recognise it.

'Speaking.'

'Ah, great. It's Janice Sawyer here from the A1 Catering Agency.'

'Hi Janice. Good to hear from you; hopefully you've had the feedback from my head chef that she's been really pleased with the staff you sent most recently.'

'Yes and we're really pleased to hear you're taking Gavin on as assistant head chef. In fact, that's why I'm calling, to confirm you're aware of the finders' fee payable to the agency?'

'Sorry, I'm not with you. Who told you we're giving Gavin a permanent role?' Even as he asked, he knew the answer. It was Lexie and she'd made her escape plan without even talking to him first.

'Your head chef, Lexie Turner; I thought you were aware of the decision?' Janice suddenly sounded flustered and it wasn't her fault that she'd just given him the worst possible news. There'd be no changing Lexie's mind, it was already too late.

'I leave those kinds of decisions to her, but I'm sure she was planning to tell me when we meet later.' Elliott didn't even know if that was true. Had she been planning to tell him? Or would she just have disappeared without saying anything. 'When's he due to start?'

'Tomorrow as I understand it and Lexie also asked for some additional temporary staffing.'

'Right, that's fine, I'm sure Lexie knows what she's doing.'

'And the finders' fee?'

'Of course. How much do we owe you?'

'It's five per cent of the first year's salary.' Janice paused. 'So by my calculations I make that two thousand pounds.'

'Just email an invoice over and I'll get it sorted. Goodbye.'

'Goodbye, Elliott, and thank you.' As he ended the call, there was a knock on the door to the office and he looked up, desperately trying to hold it together.

'Come in.'

'Sorry, the breakfast service ran a bit long this morning and I wanted to get everything ready for the picnic.' Lexie came into the office, carrying a wicker basket and looking like she didn't have a care in the world. Was it really going to be that easy for her to walk away?

'I've just had a call from the AI Catering Agency.'

'Oh.' She set the picnic down on the desk with a thud and stared at him, wordlessly. There was nothing she could say to make it better, and at least she seemed to realise that.

'When were you going to tell me you were leaving?'

'After the picnic. I just wanted us to have one last afternoon together.'

'Were you really going to tell me, or were you just going to leave?' He watched her as he spoke. 'You weren't, were you? You were just going to go without even telling me.'

'I don't know.' She turned away and looked out of the window, her back towards him. 'What does it matter anyway? We both knew I was going to go in the end. So when I went, and whether I gave you any warning of that or not, hardly matters, does it?'

'It matters to me. I thought this... whatever it is that's been going on between us, meant *something* to you. Even if it was just for the summer.'

'It was just something I needed to do. I needed a casual fling as closure to my old life, before I could move on.' She turned back to face him, her face blank. 'That's what Jasper told me.'

'Right.'

'I'm sorry, I didn't mean to hurt you. I thought you knew where we stood and I told you it was never going to be anything serious.'

'I thought I did, too, but I hadn't realised it was quite this clinical. That I was part of some kind of experiment, which was the brainchild of Jasper Holland of all people.'

'This isn't Jasper's fault. He was right, I was stuck, and I'd probably have stayed that way if it hadn't been for you, and I'll always be glad I met you. Let's just remember the summer we had and move on. Like we always planned.'

'So, when do you leave?' Elliott sat on the edge of his desk, and she ran a hand through her hair.

'Tomorrow morning.' She shrugged. 'Now that I've decided to go, I can't see the point in hanging around.'

'Have you told Billy?' If Elliott was the last to know, it wouldn't have surprised him, but she shook her head slowly. 'I wanted to wait until tomorrow, to make this afternoon and one last night all about us.'

'I think we both know that's not going to happen, don't we?' He stood up and moved back around to the other side of his desk. 'I've got a mountain of paperwork to get through and you must have packing to do.'

'Elliott, I—'

'There's nothing else you can say, really, is there? Just leave your keys with Billy in the morning.'

'I didn't want it to end this badly.'

'You wanted it to end, though, didn't you? Like you said, where and when hardly matters now.' He dropped his gaze back down to the paperwork in front of him. 'Goodbye, Lexie.'

'Bye, Elliott,' She pulled the office door shut behind her, and Elliott's head dropped into his hands. He hadn't been prepared for this, even though he'd known there was a good chance of it coming. The summer was over and nothing could change that.

11

Lexie's eyes stung and, when she looked in the mirror, the person staring back at her was someone who'd have no need for a mask on Halloween. Her eyes were bloodshot from crying for most of the night, and the dark circles beneath them underlined the fact that she'd barely slept.

It had seemed like a good idea to keep the fact that she was planning to leave a secret from Elliott until the last minute, but the look on his face had been one of pure contempt. It was like he hated her, and the speed with which he'd got her out of his office had literally taken her breath away. She knew she'd said things he didn't want to hear, things that weren't even true. But if Elliott believing he'd only ever been a gap filler meant he'd let her go without a fight, then that's what she needed to tell him.

She might have spent the night crying, but at least she wouldn't have to spend the rest of her life wondering when Elliott would be snatched away from her. Controlling when and how it ended was the only choice she could make, once she'd realised she was in love with him.

The suitcases stacked in the corner of the room looked so

insignificant compared with what they represented. It wasn't even two months since she'd arrived at Myrtle Cottage but it had been life changing, and now she was moving on again, and even Albie looked fed up at the prospect.

'Do you want some breakfast, boy?' Filling his bowl with food, she set it down on the kitchen floor and stepped back.

'Please don't tell me you hate me, too?' Lexie nudged the bowl towards him with her foot, but he just gave it a half-hearted sniff and turned his back on her again. 'How about a walk? We can go up and say goodbye to Billy and give our legs a good stretch before the long drive home.'

It was crazy talking to a dog, as if he actually understood her, as she'd done so often over the past couple of years. But when Albie spotted her unhooking the lead from the back of the kitchen door, he'd shown the first sign of anything approaching interest that he'd demonstrated all morning.

Clipping his lead on, they headed out down the path from Myrtle Cottage to the beach for what would probably be the last time. There was no way she was letting him run free today of all days, though. She didn't want to give him the chance to run off. Not when she'd promised herself that they'd be on the road by eleven at the latest to beat the high tide that would cut off the cottage for hours after that. They might even be back in London by dinner time that way. She couldn't pick up the keys to the cottage in Blackheath until the middle of September, but at least there'd be no chance of running into Elliott when they were nearly 300 miles apart. She knew she wouldn't run into him on the beach either. It was Monday morning and he'd be welcoming in a new group of guests. He'd throw himself into work, the way he always did, and his real love: life as a risk-taking adrenaline junkie. He might think he'd miss her, and she had no doubt he'd been hurt by the way she'd ended things, but he'd move on, much sooner than she would, and she was happy for him. Maybe he'd even find a woman who loved nothing better than leaping off the side of a cliff, hanging onto a bit of rope that barely looked any thicker than Albie's lead. Why couldn't she have fallen in love with someone safe this time around, boring even?

Heading across the sand with Albie, she tried to think about all the things there were to look forward to when they got back to London, but her mind kept wandering back to what was going on at the centre and whether they were coping okay without her. Suddenly Albie was barking furiously and almost pulling her arm out of its socket in his determination to move forward. Looking up, she saw an unmistakable ball of black fur hurtling towards her, the same ball of fur that had made her jump into the river in Finbar Bay. It was Splash and she was all by herself.

'Come here girl.' Lexie tried to grab hold of the little dog, as Splash and Albie greeted each other with so much enthusiasm they almost knocked her flying.

'Whatever you do, don't let her go!' A man's voice called out and, when Lexie looked up, Jasper was sprinting across the sand towards them. Hooking her hand into the dog's collar, she did as he asked.

'Thank God you got her.' For such a fitness fanatic, Jasper was breathing pretty hard by the time he reached her, so he must have run a long way. 'I told Elliott I'd look after her, but I thought he was going to end up having to rescue her too when she ran off.'

'What do you mean, "rescue her too"?' Even hearing Elliott's name hurt.

'I was in the lifeboat station, getting a few promotional shots to use on Instagram, when they got a call out. Elliott had come down for an early morning training session, before his new guests arrived, and he'd brought Splash down with him. He asked if I could look after the dog until he got back from the call out and I was at a loose end until I meet Pat for dinner later, so I said yes. I thought I'd better take the dog for a walk, but then she ran off in this direction and didn't stop until she saw you.'

'What was the call out for?' Lexie had that sense of foreboding again, like something bad was just waiting to happen. She'd never been this pessimistic before she lost Finn and she hated it.

'A young boy has disappeared from one of the holiday cottages.'

'Oh God, you don't think he's been snatched, do you?' Lexie's hand went to her mouth; the thought of something like that happening in Port Kara was impossible to believe.

'No. Apparently his parents said he was convinced about there being buried treasure on the beach, and he couldn't wait to come back out again today to find it. When they called him and his sister down to breakfast in their holiday cottage this morning, she told them he'd gone out before it was even light and that he was going to get the treasure before someone else found it.'

'They must be terrified.' Lexie couldn't even begin to imagine what the boy's poor parents were going through.

'They've had a search party combing the beach, but when they didn't find him, they decided to send out the lifeboat.'

'Is there anything we can do?' Lexie tried not to picture what might have happened to the boy if he'd got into the water. Elliott was going out to face that, though, when he knew there was a chance he could encounter any person's worst nightmare. But that was Elliott, and it was a big part of why she loved him, maybe even more than she'd loved Finn. She hadn't completely admitted it to herself until that moment, but she suddenly wanted Elliott to know it, too, more than anything. Except she'd ruined it, and now he hated her. If there'd ever been a chance for them, she'd blown it in the most spectacular way possible.

'They've got search and rescue teams going back over the beach and the cliff tops.' Jasper shrugged, as if he wished he could do more too. 'Why don't you go back and wait at the lifeboat station. I know Elliott will be happy to see you when he gets there. He'll need you, especially if the outcome is what we're all dreading.'

'He can't stand the sight of me.' She looked up at him. 'I told him what you said about just being someone who could help me move on from Finn.'

'You idiot; what did you do that for?' Jasper's words might have been blunt, but his tone was gentle.

'Because I realised I'd fallen in love with him... but you knew I would, didn't you?' The realisation hit her as she looked at him again.

'Of course I bloody did! I was just waiting for you to realise it. If I'd told you that at the start, you'd have run a mile and had nothing else to do with him.'

'And that would have hurt me less in the end.'

'Life can hurt, especially when you lose someone you love. But do you know what's worse than all of that?' She shook her head wordlessly, in response to the question. 'What's worse than all of that, is not letting yourself love anyone just to try and protect yourself from getting hurt again. If you live your life like that, Lexie, then you might as well be dead already.'

'And you only get one life.' It was almost as if she could hear Finn's voice instead of her own.

'Finn wasn't right about everything, but he was right about that, and it'd be a crime if you wasted your life hiding out from all the wonderful things you could experience, just because they aren't risk-free.' Jasper put a hand on her shoulder. 'Finn loved you, and you would probably have stayed together, but he loved himself more.'

'You can't say that!'

'I can, because it's a trait I recognise in myself. Elliott's different and, if you're really honest, you can see that too.'

'It doesn't matter, it's too late now anyway.'

'Just get over there. Take Splash back to the lifeboat station and say I gave her to you after something came up. It'll be the perfect excuse.'

'You can be all right when you try, Jasper, even if you do try to hide it sometimes.' She leant forward and kissed him on the cheek.

'I didn't think I'd ever hear you say that after what happened with Finn.'

'Me neither, but things change. Just make sure you do right by Pat, be honest with her and don't mess her around once you've had enough.'

'I wouldn't dare!'

'Just remember that.' She called back to him, already heading across the sand towards the lifeboat station. Life was too short not to take at least one risk. She couldn't leave without telling Elliott how she felt, and, if he felt the same, she wouldn't be leaving at all.

The lifeboat lurched as it hit another wave and Elliott gritted his teeth. The tide was coming in fast now and the wind was picking up, white horses dancing on the waves as the sky started to darken. It had been a glorious summer and, apart from the storm on the day they'd gone to Finbar Bay, the sky had seemed to be permanently blue and cloudless. Now there was a little boy lost somewhere, and if he'd got into the sea, just as the weather was changing for the worst, the chance of him surviving was next to nothing. The thought just piled on the misery that Elliott was already feeling, and he gripped onto the side of the boat as it rose up and down with another big wave.

'I don't think he's out here, do you? At least not anywhere we can see him.' Elliott turned to Jonty, the lifeboat helmsman, whose face looked almost as grey as the sea.

'No, I think we should head back in and let the air sea rescue helicopter scan the area, it's the best chance of us finding him if he's out here.' Jonty shook his head, an unspoken understanding passing between them. If the helicopter spotted the boy, whose name was Noah Hampshire, it almost certainly wouldn't be a happy ending. 'We could be out here for hours otherwise and it might be better if we joined the search and rescue team on the beach instead.'

'God, I hope that's where he is.' Elliott wanted to get back and join in the search as much as Jonty and the others did, but he didn't want to be on the beach when Lexie headed off from Myrtle Cottage for the last time. She'd have to leave soon, though, the tide was heading in and the way out from the cottage by car would be cut off altogether by lunch time, until the tide went out again.

'We'll find him. I know this is cutting you up, but one way or another we'll bring Noah home to his parents.' Jonty clapped Elliott on the back.

'I know.' Elliott nodded. Jonty didn't need to hear that Noah wasn't the only thing on his mind. His problems were tiny in comparison to what the boy's parents were going through, but that didn't stop him from hating the thought of Lexie leaving for good.

Lexie almost broke into a run as she got within sight of the lifeboat station; she was so close and not even the thought of having to admit to Elliott why she'd said those awful things to him could put her off. She was almost level with the network of caves that hollowed out the cliffs underneath Dagger's Head, when Splash suddenly jerked violently to the right and slipped out of her lead. Lexie threw herself forward to try and catch the little dog, but

Splash was too quick and, within seconds, she'd disappeared into the caves.

'Oh for God's sake!' Lexie was beginning to wonder if Splash had preferred being a stray; she seemed so determined to escape at every opportunity. But if she didn't get her back, and soon, there was a real danger that the incoming tide would fill up the cave and Splash might not survive her encounter with the water this time around.

As Lexie reached the mouth of the cave, Albie began to pull on his lead too, dragging her in before she had time to think about whether it was safe to do so. Trying to keep hold of him, and clamber across the slippery dark grey rocks, was almost impossible. He started barking as the rocks led upwards and deeper into the cave, and she had to decide whether to turn back. There was a tunnel on the left hand side, which she knew from talking to Elliott led into a network of other tunnels that had apparently been used by smugglers for hundreds of years. On the right hand side was a dead end, where the rocks were more jagged and vicious, but Albie seemed determined to go that way, his deep bark echoing off the walls.

'She can't be up there.' Lexie tried to tug him in the other direction. If the worst came to the worst, at least if they were in the tunnel they could keep climbing and stay out of the water. Eventually the other end of the tunnel would open out to a crevice in a patch of woodland on the clifftop. It was a treacherous climb by all accounts, but at least they wouldn't drown. And if they couldn't make it to the top, they could at least wait it out until the tide went back out. If they took the dead end on the right, they'd be completely cut off by the tide and only a complete idiot would risk that.

Suddenly there was a much more high-pitched bark coming from the dead end to the right of where they were standing, and all attempts to persuade Albie into the tunnel on the left were off. He pulled away from her, his lead slipping out of her hand, and she had no choice but to clamber up the rocks and follow him towards where Splash had obviously gone. If that made her an idiot, then that's what she was. But, when it came to it, she couldn't leave Albie or Splash, even if it meant taking the biggest risk she'd ever taken. She had cuts all over her hands and legs by the time she reached the ledge that Albie had stopped on.

Peering into the darkness beyond the ledge, she spotted some movement. It had to be Splash. At least she hoped it was; if there was something else in there, she wasn't sure she wanted to know. Not that she believed in the local legends about witches and the ghosts of long-dead smugglers, but she was terrified enough as it was by the prospect of not being able to get out of the cave again.

'Come on Splash, don't be scared.' Lexie could hear the desperation in her own voice, so it probably wouldn't do anything to reassure the dog. 'Here girl, come on.'

'She's shivering; I think she's really frightened.' Lexie nearly lost her footing as she stepped back in disbelief. Whoever owned the voice sounded young, very young, and pretty terrified himself. She was so shocked, it took her a few seconds to realise it must be the missing boy, who Elliott was out searching for. She wished Jasper had known the boy's name, it would make this next bit much easier.

'I'm sure she's frightened. I'm just glad you're there to look after her. My name's Lexie, and hers is Splash, I've got my dog, Albie, here as well.'

'I'm Noah.' His voice shook as he said his name. 'And I'm scared too.'

'It'll be okay, Noah, I promise. I'm going to get you and Splash out of here. Are you hurt?'

'I don't think so; I've cut my legs, but I think I'm okay.'

'That's good, Noah. How did you get up here?' It was a stupid question, there was only one way he could have got up there, but what she really wanted to know was *why*.

'I wanted to look for treasure and I thought I'd find it in the cave, but then I got too scared to climb down again.' Noah started to sniff, finally giving in to the tears that he'd obviously been holding in. 'I'm going to be in so much trouble.'

'No you won't, sweetheart.' Lexie fought to keep her own voice steady. 'Everyone just wants to make sure you're safe.'

'Some men came and they were shouting my name, but I was too scared to answer them.'

'Don't worry, I'm here now and I promise I'm not scary. Albie really wants to meet you, too; he's Splash's best friend.' Lexie felt in her jeans' pocket. Thank goodness her mobile was still there. Once it illuminated, it was obvious there was no signal, but at least she could use the torch. Pointing it forward, she could see the narrow ledge that led to a wide platform where Splash was sitting on Noah's lap. He had tousled brown hair and a face so pale that he could easily have played the part of a ghostly smuggler. 'Do you want me to come to you, or do you want to come back to me, if I shine the torch on to the ledge?'

'I'll come to you; I don't want us both to get stuck here.' Noah's voice had a new determination and he lifted Splash off his lap, standing up slowly.

'When you get to the edge of the ledge, I'll throw the end of one of the dog leads towards you and you can tie that around your wrist, so that there's no way you can fall.' Lexie waited as Noah and Splash made their way to the edge of the narrowest part of the ledge. Splash trotted across towards her, as sure-footed as if she was just running across the sand, and Noah looked straight at Lexie.

'I'm still scared.'

'I promise I won't let anything happen to you.' Lexie forced herself to smile, hoping she didn't look as much like a shop mannequin as she felt. 'Okay, catch hold of the other end of the lead when I throw it over.'

It took three attempts before Noah finally managed to catch the end of the lead. Thankfully, Splash's lead was the type that combined a collar and automatically tightened to fit when you pulled on it. So all Noah had to do was slip the end over his wrist.

'I've done it. I'm ready.' The young boy nodded, his face already strained with concentration.

'Well done, sweetheart. Just take it really slowly and steadily. There's no rush.' Lexie held her breath, almost as tightly as she was gripping the other end of the lead. His foot slipped when he was about three feet away from her, but he righted himself at the same time as she reached out to grab him and pulled him into her arms, both of them falling back on to the rocks behind her.

'I'm sorry.' Noah really started to sob and she was terrified he'd hurt himself in the fall.

'Are you okay, sweetheart?'

'Y-y-yes.' He got the word out eventually and for a moment she just held on to him. Both of the dogs were nudging them, making their own attempt to reassure Noah and Lexie that everything would be okay.

'You did so brilliantly getting back across here. All we've got to do now is get back down to the bottom of the cave and then we can go and find your mum and dad.'

'You promise they won't be mad at me?' Noah looked up at her and smiled, this time for real.

'They'll be so happy to see you, nothing else will matter. Come on then, let's get back down to the beach.'

They picked their way steadily down the rocks, with Lexie leading the way and holding out her hand to help Noah down when he needed it. Both the dogs were off their leads now and they were much more able to navigate the slippery rocks, and the even more dangerous gaps between them, than Noah and Lexie were. But eventually they got to a flatter part of the cave. It was obvious then that the water level was rising; the dogs had stopped moving, and, when Lexie stepped down again, she was immediately thigh high in water. This time it was Noah who held out a hand and pulled her back up out of the water.

'What are we going to do now?'

'We're going to wait here until someone comes and helps us get out, or until the tide goes out again. It'll be okay whatever happens, I promise.' Just as Lexie made Noah yet another promise she wasn't sure she could keep, a huge fork of lightning lit up the sky. A storm was on its way and she had no idea just how high the water level might rise. They might have to climb up the rocks again to where they'd started, but it had been wet and slippery up there too and she had no way of knowing whether there was anywhere that would be safe to wait the storm out. Noah didn't need to know that, though; all she could do now was keep him safe for as long as possible and try to stop him realising how terrified she felt.

'I'm glad you're here, Lexie.' Noah leant up against her and she put her arm around his shoulder, watching the waves crashing onto the rocks below them.

'I'm glad I'm here too, Noah.' Hugging him to her, she realised she meant it. Whatever the risk to her, she wanted to be there for Noah and, in that moment, she understood Elliott better than she ever had before. She just wished he was there too; there was no one else she wanted.

* * *

When they got back to the lifeboat station, Elliott was praying that the little boy who'd disappeared would have been found safe and well, but a call had come through on the radio just as they arrived back to say that there were still no positive sightings of the missing child. The tide had now come in all the way, and there was just a narrow half-moon of sand at the lifeboat station end of the beach, which allowed access to the coastal path. The stretch of beach that ran from Dagger's Head to Myrtle Cottage was now completely cut off by the tide.

'The search and rescue team are concentrating on the cliffs now.' Jonty came into the kit room, as Elliott and the others were getting changed and ready to join in the land-based rescue efforts. 'They think they'd have found him by now, if he'd still been on the beach, and if he isn't somewhere on the cliffs…' Jonty didn't need to finish the sentence.

Elliott took his mobile phone out of the locker to check whether any of the guides, who were working with the search and rescue team, had sent him a message. But there was only one message, and it was from Lexie.

I don't think you'll get this because there's no signal on my phone. I tried to call you and it wouldn't connect. But if they find my phone afterwards, I wanted you to be able to read this. I'm sorry Elliott for everything. I didn't mean what I said. I love you. More than I've loved anyone. I found Noah, but we're trapped in the cave at Dagger's Head. Both the dogs are with us. Please forgive me xxx

'I know where they are.' Elliott dropped the phone onto the bench beside him, already starting to pull his kit back on. 'Lexie's in the cave at Dagger's Head, with Noah, and they've been cut off by the tide. The way this storm is closing in, the water level could rise all the way to the top of the cave if we don't get there.'

'Your Lexie?' Jonty's eyes widened when Elliott nodded. She was his, and he had to get to her. 'I'll alert the helicopter team, they might need to winch them to safety, but we'll relaunch the boat as soon as the crew's ready.'

The rest of the crew moved just as quickly as Elliott, everyone caught up in the sense of urgency that had filled the room. A loud rumble of thunder, as the boat sped down the launch, was just another reminder of how bad things were. The waves were already twice as high as they had been when they'd got back to the lifeboat station and the sky was almost black with rain that seemed to be driving horizontally as well as vertically. It was vicious weather.

Elliott couldn't have spoken to the others, even if he'd been able to hear what they were saying over the sound of the roaring sea. Leaning his back against the wall of the boat, he just kept praying that he'd reach Lexie in time and have a chance to say all the things he so badly wanted to say. The things he'd been holding back since the moment they'd met. He'd told himself that it was moving too fast, and that they didn't know each other well enough to have fallen in love – especially when what he did know about her suggested they couldn't be more different. But life didn't follow a set of rules, where matching people's interests could guarantee you the perfect relationship. You were just supposed to grab it with both hands and be thankful it had found you. He'd never shied away from taking a risk. So why had he done it when the stakes were at their highest?

'The cliff opening is just up ahead, but we're not going to be able to get the boat in all the way, not with the waves bringing on water the way they are.' Jonty was still having to shout to be heard. 'We should just wait here on standby, until the helicopter can winch them up, in case they need us.'

'I can't just sit here and wait, Jonty. Not when I know they're in there.'

'Elliott, you can't, it's too dangerous.' Even as he spoke, Jonty was pulling out a length of rope. They both knew that Elliott was going to do it anyway, so they might as well make it as safe as they could. The helicopter had been called out on another emergency, just before they'd relaunched the lifeboat, and there was no way of knowing how long it would take before they got there.

'If you get the boat as close to the mouth of the cave as you can, I'll go in, you can tether the rope to me and I'll bring them back one by one. If we wait for the helicopter, it could be too late.' Elliott was already tying the rope around his waist, as Jonty secured the other end to the boat.

'What if we wait five minutes?' He had to hand it to Jonty, he was giving it a shot, but Elliott shook his head.

'I'm sorry mate, I just can't wait.' He double-checked his life jacket and the one he was taking with him to bring Noah back to the boat. Lexie would have to wait until he came back for her, unless the helicopter beat him to it.

'Good luck, buddy.' Jonty clapped his hand on Elliott's shoulder again, as he passed him, and seconds later he was in the water. They'd managed to get the boat to the mouth of the cave, so it shouldn't have taken him long to swim in, but with waves crashing against the rocks and the wind making the tidal flow fight against itself, it was much more of a battle than it should have been. Eventually he made it inside the cave, out of the wind and lashing rain, and it got a bit easier to swim.

'Lexie! Noah!' Shouting into the cave, his voice echoed off the walls and for a moment he didn't hear anything, but then he heard a voice that was like music to his ears.

'Elliott, we're up here.' Looking up, he could see them on a ledge, about six feet above where the water had risen to. Swimming over, so he was directly below them, he called up again.

'I'm going to throw this life-jacket up to you, Lexie, and I want you to put it on Noah and make sure it's properly secured. Then Noah's going to need to jump into the water, so I can get him out of here and back onto the boat. When I've done that, I'll come back for you.'

'Okay.' Lexie didn't even question it or ask how he'd found them. There was so much he wanted to tell her, and a million promises he wanted to make, but now wasn't the time. The only promise he needed to fulfil right now was that he would come back for her.

Taking his arm back as far as he could, he threw the life jacket up and, for once, luck seemed to be on their side. Lexie caught the jacket and he could just about hear her reassuring Noah as she fastened the ties around him, and made sure he was ready to go into the water.

'Everything okay up there?'

'Noah's ready, but he's a bit scared. I've told him you'll look after him, Elliott, and that I trust you more than anyone I've ever met.'

'Lexie's right, I promise I'll look after you, Noah. You just have to be a brave boy one more time and jump into the water when Lexie tells you to.'

'I'm going to count to three.' Lexie's tone was forceful. 'One, two, three…' Almost before she'd got to the final number, there was a splash, just a few feet away from Elliott. Swimming over, he could see the little boy's face more clearly, and he looked absolutely terrified.

'It's all right Noah, I'm here now and in a few more minutes we'll be back at the boat.'

'Lexie pushed me, but I know she had to, or I'd never have jumped.'

'She was just helping you.' Elliott used the extra length of rope he'd left hanging loose, and tied Noah to him, so that there was no way they could be separated when they left the protection of the cave. Taking up the slack on the other end of the rope until it was tight, he yanked it hard three times, to let Jonty know he was ready to be pulled in. The progress they made back to the boat was far quicker with the help of the crew and, within minutes, Noah had been lifted into the safety of the boat.

'Are you sure you can make it back?' Jonty had barely got the words out and passed another life jacket over the side, before Elliott began to swim away from the boat in the direction of the cave again, without even answering. It was harder still this time, but the thought of getting Lexie back to safety drove him on. When he got back to her, he called up again.

'I'm going to throw another life jacket up and then you just need to do what Noah did and jump in.'

'I can't.'

'Of course you can; I'm here and I won't let anything happen to you.' It was the same promise he'd made to Noah.

'I know, but I can't leave the dogs here.'

'I'll come back for them, after I've made sure you're safely on the boat.'

'They'll never jump into the water willingly. I can't leave Albie here, or Splash. I'm sorry.'

'There's no point me arguing with you, is there?' His voice was getting tight from shouting, and swallowing water as he'd powered through the waves to get to her and Noah.

'No, sorry.'

'Right, when I throw the life jacket up, put it on Albie as best you can and then push him in. I'll get him back to the boat and then I'll come back for you and Splash. She's light enough for you to hold in your arms.' It took two attempts for Lexie to catch the life jacket this time and getting it on Albie proved more difficult than getting a life jacket onto Noah had, judging by the amount of reassurance she had to give the dog. Eventually, there was a loud splash and Elliott swam over to him. Albie wasn't nearly as compliant as Noah either and he struggled all the way back to the boat, trying to get away from Elliott, as if he held him personally responsible for the predicament he'd found himself in. Even with the rest of the crew pulling on the rope to get them back to the boat, it was exhausting.

'The bloody dog?' Jonty was incredulous when he hauled Albie on to the boat.

'She wouldn't come without them.' Elliott's words were coming out in gasps, and he was desperately fighting to get his breathing back into some sort of a rhythm. 'I need another life jacket.'

'You can't go back again, mate, seriously. One of us will have to do it.' Jonty held out his arm to pull Elliott back into the boat, but he turned away towards the cave again.

'I'm not getting out, so just chuck me the life jacket. Please.'

'You're insane.' Despite his words, Jonty threw a life jacket and it landed just in front of him.

'It's got to be me that goes. Good throw by the way.' Maybe he was being stupid and risking both their lives, but he had to be the one to bring her back. He loved her and he didn't trust anyone else to fight as hard as he would to save her life. The burning sensation in his lungs was agony as he swam against the violent waves, but nothing would stop him whilst he still had breath in his body.

'I'm here.' Elliott called up again, his throat raw with the effort of so much shouting. The light that had illuminated the ledge, where Lexie had been standing, had gone out.

'The battery on my phone has died.' Hearing her voice in the dark, relief flooded his body.

'It's about to get very wet in a minute, anyway. I don't think a bag of rice is going to be able to salvage it after this.'

'I sent you a message, but there was no signal.'

'I got it, that's how I found you. It must have picked up a signal briefly at some point.'

'I meant what I said, I'm sorry.'

'I know, but you don't need to worry about any of that now.' He wanted to tell her he loved her too, but it felt like he would be jinxing things if he did. If he didn't say the words to her now, they both had to get back to the boat safely so he could tell her how he felt. 'I'm going to throw a life jacket up again, but it's going to be hard, because I can't see you any more. So I need you to sing.'

'You're joking.'

'I'm deadly serious.'

'But I can't hold a note!' Her words were accompanied by a slightly hysterical laugh.

'Don't worry, it's not Britain's Got Talent.' Elliott waited and then she suddenly started to sing.

'Sorry, but this is all I can think of! *Silent night, holy night, all is calm, all is bright...*' As she sang the lyrics to the Christmas carol, Elliott took aim, throwing the life jacket and waiting for her to shout that it had missed her by miles and she couldn't see it. He wasn't sure he'd be able to go and get another one and make it back to her, he could barely feel his arms and legs as it was.

'I've got it!' Lexie sounded almost as euphoric as he felt.

'Brilliant, put it on and make sure it's secured and then jump in with Splash in your arms.' It felt like an eternity until she answered him.

'I'm ready.' She didn't wait for him to answer, and he heard her hit the water. Any second and he was actually going to be able to reach out and touch her.

'Where are you?'

'Just to your left, I think. But Splash isn't happy.'

Swimming towards the sound of her voice, they were almost face to face before he finally made out her shape in the darkness.

'Do you think you can keep hold of her?' Elliott already had a hand looped through one of the straps on her life jacket. He wasn't going to let her go again.

'I think so.'

'Good. I'll tie you to me and then all you've got to do is hold on to Splash, then the crew will pull us all in.' Even Elliott's hands didn't seem to want to cooperate as he tied a final knot in the rope and pulled it in tight again, giving three last yanks to let the crew know they were ready to be pulled back in. Wrapping his arms around Lexie and Splash, he felt some of the tension leave his spine as they began to be dragged in the direction of the boat.

Untying Lexie and Splash, when they finally reached the side of the lifeboat, Jonty and the others dragged them on board, and then hauled Elliott over the side, just as a helicopter passed overhead.

'Are you okay?' Lexie threw her arms around him, as Splash tried to get in between them, licking his face.

'I am now.' He pulled her towards him, not caring what the rest of the crew made of their reunion. If he'd had enough breath left in his lungs, he'd have shouted what he said next against the howling wind. 'I love you, too.'

'I've been such an idiot. I don't care about the fact that you take risks for a living, I just want to be with you for as long as we're given. Like you said, no one knows how long they've got anyway, and we'll make the most of every day.'

'I'm not going anywhere, I've got too much to lose now.' Elliott hoped she'd heard him but, with the boat racing back to shore, he couldn't be certain. It didn't matter, though, they had the rest of their lives together, and he was going to tell her every day just how much she meant to him.

EPILOGUE

The flowers around the door outside the Sailor's Chapel, by the harbour in Port Kara, were just as Lexie had imagined they'd be. The florist had promised to use the same wild flowers that grew on the cliffs where she'd first met Elliott, and in less than twenty-four hours she'd be walking through the arch – on her father's arm – and down the aisle to where Elliott would be waiting. Billy was going to be his best man, and her bridesmaids – Morwenna, Vyvyan, Pat and Billy's girlfriend, Aisha – had a combined age of over two hundred years. It might not be traditional, but she wouldn't have had it any other way.

'It's hard to believe that this time last year, we didn't even know each other's names.' Lexie kept her hand in Elliott's as they stopped by the edge of the harbour, to take a last look at the chapel, before they went their separate ways and spent the night before the wedding apart. She was going to be staying at Jasper Holland's house, where Pat seemed to have permanently moved in after Jory and Vyvyan had got engaged at Christmas. Lexie wouldn't have believed any of it when she'd decided to spend the summer in Port Kara, but Morwenna had been right all along. She said Lexie would know when she'd found the place she was meant to be, and it had taken being stranded in the darkness of a cave for her to finally see the light.

'It is hard to believe, but I can't imagine my life without you in it. Are you sure Port Kara's going to be enough for you?' He grinned, and she nodded in response.

'As long as you don't think we're too different to make it any more?'

'I'm a risk taker, you know that.'

'Don't take any unnecessary chances tonight, though, will you?' Lexie raised an eyebrow. 'If Billy and the others take you out for a last night of freedom, you could end up tied to a lamp post with your eyebrows shaved off.'

'I don't need a last night of freedom, tomorrow can't come fast enough.' Elliott couldn't seem to stop smiling.

'It'll be brilliant to see Noah again, too.' The little boy whose rescue had brought them together was going to be a ring bearer at the wedding, and even Albie and Splash were allowed into the chapel.

'I know you're probably fed up with hearing this, but I love you Lexie Turner.'

'I think I can put up with hearing it, if you can put up with me saying it back?' She tilted her face, and he didn't need words to answer her. Finn had been right, you only got one life, and a Cornish summer's kiss had changed hers for good.

ACKNOWLEDGMENTS

A huge thank you to all of the team at Boldwood Books. With special gratitude to my brilliant editor, Emily, and to Candida for her excellent copyediting and proofreading skills.

Another massive thank you goes to everyone who reads my books and especially those who take the time to leave a review, including the amazing book blogging community.

This book is dedicated to the family and friends who have given me high days and holidays that will live in my memory forever. Thank you all for your love and friendship.

Finally, as always, the biggest thank you goes to my family for their patience, support and belief in me.

MORE FROM JO BARTLETT

We hope you enjoyed reading *A Cornish Summer's Kiss*. If you did, please leave a review.

If you'd like to gift a copy, this book is also available as an ebook, digital audio download and audiobook CD.

Sign up to Jo Bartlett's mailing list for news, competitions and updates on future books.

http://bit.ly/JoBartlettNewsletter

Why not explore the top 10 bestselling The Cornish Midwives series:

ABOUT THE AUTHOR

Jo Bartlett is the bestselling author of nineteen women's fiction titles. She fits her writing in between her two day jobs as an educational consultant and university lecturer and lives with her family and three dogs on the Kent coast.

Visit Jo's Website: www.jobartlettauthor.com

 twitter.com/J_B_Writer
 facebook.com/JoBartlettAuthor
 instagram.com/jo_bartlett123

ABOUT BOLDWOOD BOOKS

Boldwood Books is a fiction publishing company seeking out the best stories from around the world.

Find out more at www.boldwoodbooks.com

Sign up to the Book and Tonic newsletter for news, offers and competitions from Boldwood Books!

http://www.bit.ly/bookandtonic

We'd love to hear from you, follow us on social media:

facebook.com/BookandTonic
twitter.com/BoldwoodBooks
instagram.com/BookandTonic

Printed in Great Britain
by Amazon